THE
FUNERAL PROCESSION

THE
FUNERAL
PROCESSION

A Novel by

ANEEK CHATTERJEE

PARTRIDGE

ISBN: Softcover   978-1-4828-5154-0
            eBook   978-1-4828-5153-3

[Although many parts of this novel are inspired by real events, all characters in the story are imaginary, and bear no resemblance with any person, living or dead. This novel is about humanity and peace, and does not intend to hurt, at any point of story-telling, any sentiments.]

Because of the dynamic nature of the Internet, any web addresses or links contained in this book may have changed since publication and may no longer be valid. The views expressed in this work are solely those of the author and do not necessarily reflect the views of the publisher, and the publisher hereby disclaims any responsibility for them.

Print information available on the last page.

To order additional copies of this book, contact
Partridge India
000 800 10062 62
orders.india@partridgepublishing.com

www.partridgepublishing.com/india

Contents

1

THE FUNERAL PROCESSION

The June sun was merciless over this small sub-divisional town. Beside the boundary wall of the 'Pir Baba's graveyard, under the Deodar tree, six little boys were playing 'Charrac', - a game played with marbles by drawing a 'court' on the ground. Today being Monday, there was no visitor to the Pir Baba's graveyard. Usually devotees thronged the graveyard on Fridays with flowers and small earthen replica of animals, - horses or bulls,- singed and browned,- for prayers. They placed flowers and burnt earthen pieces on the graveyard and chanted prayers. The little boys only watched with wonder. After the departure of the devotees, they used to collect the horses and bulls. Even a year ago J and his friends did not dare to touch the animals, because Sona-da[*]* told that black spirits usually descended upon these earthen animals. So they dared not touch them and watched helplessly as other para (locality) boys collected

---

[*] Usually the suffix 'da' is added in Bengal for a moderately senior and older man; and 'di' for a moderately older woman. Thus 'Sona-da' refers to a person whose name is actally 'Sona'.

them and played with those earthen animals. Now J, aged seven years, and his friends had realized that no harm was done if they played with the brown earthen animals.

There were no devotees at the 'Pir baba's grave today. The boys were relaxed and deeply engrossed in the 'charrac' game. J was targeting the green marble in the 'charrac court' with the golden one in his hand when Pancha-da appeared and told slowly but seriously, "Go home J, your father is no more". J paused for a while, stared vacantly at Panchada's face and then threw his marble. It hit the green one in the court. J jumped with joy. Now the green marble would be his; his stock of marbles would increase to thirty, J calculated in his mind. His friends could no longer participate in the game. With uneasiness in their faces, they gave the green marble to J and stopped playing. Now Panchada said harshly, "Go home J, your father is dead". Some dry yellow leaves fell from the deodar tree on the Charrac Court at that moment. J looked up; the sky was burning in this early June morning. J began to run and reached home within two minutes.

Outside his house, the 'Para dadas', - senior boys of the locality, - were levelling bamboo sticks. J realized that the para boys were preparing the last bed for his father. Earlier he had seen such hand-made bamboo beds in funeral processions. Inside, there was an uproarious scene that J never watched before. Mother was crying loudly, and J's three elder sisters joined her. Barda (eldest brother), with tears in his eyes, was whispering something to Sitaram-da, his friend. Fulda and Bhai (fifth and sixth elder brothers to J) were also weeping. Father was sleeping calmly on the floor. Around him several men and women, some known, some unknown, gathered. Chhordi (second elder sister) was crying loudly. J was confused, and could not realize what to do. Nobody was paying any attention to J.

Everybody was observing the crying party, - mother and her three daughters. J looked at father's face. It appeared that father was trying to say something. J could hardly remember father saying anything anytime. He used to sit on a wooden chair occasionally. But most of the time, he was in his bed. Barda said he was paralytic, and Chhordi was his full-time aya-cum-nurse, from morning to night, washing linens, supplying meals and bed pan, combing his hair, and wiping tears that often rolled down his cheeks. J had one single, just one single image of father, - sitting like a child in his wooden chair in the winter sun. J never talked to him, because father could not talk. J had realized that father's gestures were only understood by Barda, Mother and Chhordi. These were not meant for others. Although father watched him play from his wooden chair, J used to avoid him. Now J looked intensely at father's face. He was sure father wanted to say something. What, J did not understand. If only Barda, Chhordi or Mother could see! They would have surely understood what father was trying to say. But Mother and Chhordi were still crying, and Barda was running here and there, trying to arrange post-death formalities.

Barda told Sankar-da (a family friend) to telegram Didi, Chhorda, Mejda, and Fagun, - J's eldest sister and three elder brothers. Didi had been staying in faraway Assam. Her husband, a lower division railway clerk, was posted there for many years. Mejda, the second son in the family after Barda, left home in his adolescence in search of jobs. He knew a little typing, and his friends told him that typists were in great demand with private companies in Calcutta.

Mejda went to Calcutta and settled in a very small room in a dingy locality. Chhorda, the third son, applied for a job in the Indian Army and after drill and physical fitness test in a local ground, got the job. He was frequently transferred to different places of India. He was recently posted at Almorah, a small town in the Himalayas. Fagun, the fourth son of the family, joined Bengal Police and was posted at Purulia, a district far off from J's hometown, bordering Bihar. For reasons unknown to J, everybody in the family, from seniors to juniors, called him 'Fagun', his nick name. J had six elder brothers and four elder sisters. He was the youngest in a family of eleven children.

Barda told Sankarda to take the family bicycle for the Telegraph Office. J was watching Sankarda's movements. As he went out for the bicycle, J silently slipped out of the crying party and requested Sankarda to take him along. Sankarda hesitated initially, but agreed. J sat on the front iron rod of the cycle as Sankar paddled his way to the Telegraph Office. They did not talk. The Telegraph Office, J realized was a busy place. Sankar gave a piece of paper to the clerk at the counter. The clerk looked through Sankar-da and read out the message, probably for verification, and J heard: FATHER EXPIRED, COME SOON. Sankarda nodded. The clerk then said, "Address". Sankarda gave four more pieces of paper: Assam, Calcutta, Almorah and Purulia. It took nearly half an hour to complete the formalities. J was watching people throughout the time, inside the office and on the adjacent road. The din and bustle inside the office was in stark contrast to the almost empty road outside. Very few people ventured out in the mid-day June Sun. Some rickshaw pullers sat lazily in their cycle-rickshaws under a big tree opposite the Telegraph Office. They were wiping sweats with their napkins as they waited for passengers. J was also keeping an eye on their family bicycle which was parked just outside the big window in front of the counter. Sankarda said, "Keep an eye, now-a-days cycle thieves are on a spree". A suspicious looking man with long beards was approaching the cycle a few minutes ago. J became stiff. But thank God, he entered the office and went to a counter! Sankarda said finally, "let's get back". It was a long journey back home under a blazing sun. Sankarda said, "Try to remember this date forever J, never forget this date. Your father died today, the 6th of June, 1969".

*   *   *

The bamboo bed was ready. It was waiting in the small ground-like area located at the entrance of the house. The para dadas were chatting under the custard apple tree. When Sankarda and J were about to enter the house, Sonada told Sankarda, "Ask Barda when the funeral party would start". Sankar nodded and went inside with J. The howl had stopped, but occasional sobs from J's sisters could be heard. Father was on the floor, and the crowd around him had become much thinner. Only close friends of J's brothers and sisters stayed back. J saw Barda busy discussing the possible time for the funeral procession with some of the elders of the locality. Some opined that they should wait for other brothers to reach town, but others said that would be too late. It would take at least seven hours for Mejda to arrive from the city, - the nearest location. Since the funeral ground had poor lighting arrangements, some elders suggested that it would be better to reach there before evening. It was decided to start early, preferably after lunch.

Sankar-da communicated the message to the para youths. They went to their respective homes for lunch. It was 1 p.m. and J was feeling very hungry. But he knew that there would be no meal in his house today. Only tea was allowed in a house where someone had died. The elders were already served tea. J thought that he would ask Mother for food, but could not muster enough courage. Instead he went to the kitchen and found Chhordi with some para ladies. One elderly lady said, "Such a little boy; lost his father so early in his life", and started crying. Chhordi also joined her. J got puzzled and irritated. He was about to leave the kitchen when another lady said,

"He must be hungry; give him some food".

One young lady said, "Custom prevents any food till the funeral is over".

The elderly one said, "God does not take any objection if food is taken by the little ones".

The younger one replied, "But the spirit of his father would be angry if he takes food".

J now became interested in the conversation. How did a spirit look like? Would the spirit of his father look like his own actual father? J closed his eyes to remember how his father looked like. The image of a paralytic crippled man sitting on a wooden chair in the winter sun appeared before his closed eyes. Would the spirit also sit on the wooden chair, crippled? How a crippled spirit would prevent him from taking food? One of his friends told him the other day that spirits could do anything anywhere anytime. Spirits were very powerful. What magic could make the spirit of a paralytic man so powerful? J became curious. He would consult his friends over this issue, he decided. Meanwhile the para ladies came to a conclusion. God was superior to spirits. So if God allowed food for the little ones, spirits could not intervene and cause any harm. Satisfied by this verdict, Chhordi gave him two hand-made breads with 'gur' (molasses). J swiftly ate the breads, and had a glass of water. The hunger was finally over.

The funeral party started after 2 p.m. Before the departure, a photograph was taken with J, Mother, Barda, three sisters, Fulda and Bhai sitting around father's last bed. J was very happy because Barda told him to do an important duty in the funeral procession. J would walk in front of the procession and scatter perched rice throughout the route of the procession. J had seen many funeral processions already. The rich people of the town scattered coins with perched rice, called "khoi" in this area, in the funeral processions. J and his friends followed several such processions for coins. But once the processions crossed their locality, they had to stop following; it was now the turn of boys from other localities to collect coins. This was the rule of the game. The stronger ones sometimes dared to follow the processions all along inviting challenges from other para boys. But J never crossed his own locality. Barda gave him a big paper packet full of white khoi, and asked him to scatter miserly, a few khoi at a time, so that the packet lasted till the funeral ground which was far away from J's house. J knew that they were poor. So he decided to scatter the perched rice judiciously.

The bamboo bed was lifted. Huge cries, louder than the earlier, filled the air. Barda and Bhai gave their shoulders in front, Fulda and Sonada at the rear. Other para youths followed. Ladies stayed back. The funeral ground was far away, and the sun was blazing. Moreover, custom in this town did not allow ladies to walk in funeral processions.

After nearly every kilometer, shoulders would change, but at least one son among the four bearers of the last bed would have to give his shoulder throughout the journey. Barda, Fulda and Bhai would alternate among them later. J was scattering 'khoi' infront. He watched with joy that his friends noticed him in the act. They never got such a chance. J felt very proud.

It was customary for funeral parties to chant "Balo Hari, Hari Bol" (Say God, say God), and this party was no exception. For the first time in his small life J discovered that this chanting had a sweet rhythm within it. First some people would chant "Balo Hari", and then others would murmur "Hari Bol". This would go on like a well-rehearsed orchestrated rhythm throughout the journey. J also chanted "Balo Hari, Hari Bol". It was pious to utter these words in the funeral procession, elders said.

The party reached the funeral ground at around 5 p.m. Everybody was sweating profusely. The place was a big one by the side of the river Ganga. At the far end of the ground stood some concrete structure, which J realized, was the 'office' of this burning ghat. At one end of the concrete structure, huge stocks of wooden pieces were piled up. A tough-faced man was sitting nearby and smoking 'biri'. Some other men, probably 'Doms' (those who helped in the funeral, normally downtrodden in society), were loitering here and there. By the river side, a pyre was still burning, and a 'Dom' was searching something in the pyre with a sharp long bamboo stick. This attracted J's attention. He went closer to the pyre. The 'Dom' shouted loudly, "What are you up to? Don't go that much closer". J retreated and watched silently. Was the Dom searching for the navel of the dead man? J's friends told him that navels did not burn, and the Doms used to eat half-burnt navels with country liquor. This extraordinary food was the reason behind their powerful bodies. With curly hairs, big moustache, and strong arms, they were like demons.

Sonada appeared and rebuked, "You are here? Every body's searching for you. Come with me". J went with Sonada to the other side of the funeral ground. Father was laid under a Tamarind tree. The elders bought wood-pieces from the 'office', and a few men were busy preparing the pyre. The 'official' priest arrived. He ordered somebody to bring a pot of 'sacred' Ganga water and mud from the river bank. He placed the pot on the mud and lit incensed sticks. J was watching curiously. The priest asked Barda to come closer, and murmured some holy verses. Thereafter, he asked Barda to sprinkle some water on Father. Now he shouted, "Where is the youngest son?" Everyone pointed towards J. Somebody from the crowd said, "Leave the youngest son; he is too small to light the pyre". The priest said sternly, "That is the ritual; if you want to break the custom, the dead man will be unhappy, even furious". No one protested any more.

The wooden pieces were stacked in an orderly manner by the groundsmen. Father was laid above the wooden pieces when these reached some height. Then again the groundsmen started placing pieces of wood over Father's body. J wondered how Father was bearing so much weight! Dead people really gathered strength that no living person could ever possess!

Finally, the pyre was ready. The Priest walked a single round along the pyre with Barda. He then asked Barda, J and other sons to walk seven rounds. The Priest lighted a long piece of wood and handed it over to Barda, before the sons started their rounds. He chanted holy verses when J and his brothers were doing the rounds. When seven rounds were completed, Barda, as the eldest son, lighted the pyre, and handed over the burning piece of wood to J, the youngest son, as per custom. J felt the heat, but held the piece firmly and moved it closer to the pyre. Then Fulda took it from him, and finally Bhai took the wooden piece from Fulda. Soon the pyre was in flames. The funeral crowd retreated and watched the pyre from a distance. J slipped away from the crowd and slowly went to the almost empty road high above the funeral ground. From there he could see all the men, and the pyre that was burning furiously, with black thick smoke billowing from the fire. Was father's spirit moving up to the sky along with the black smoke? Could his father see him standing alone in this place, from his house of smoke? J tried to remember Father. The wooden chair in the winter sun appeared again with a crippled, unshaved child-like man seated on it. Father was long dead to J, he died today.

2

NAXALS AND THE SHOP-SCHOOL

On a sultry September morning, nearly three months after father's death, Barda came from the market, parked his bicycle and announced grimly, "B.P. Saha has been killed by the Naxals".

"B.P. Saha, the grocer?" asked Chhordi, "such a nice person; like a grandpa, why did the Naxals kill him?" she looked sad. Barda too was on a pensive mood.

"I am thinking on a different line", he said, "who would lend us essential goods on credit now? From whom shall we buy on credit rice, wheat, pulses, soap, detergent …"

Now Chhordi started crying. The shock of not getting essentials pained her more than Bishnu Pada Saha's death, J could understand.

But who were these Naxals? J heard that they were good people; they were for the poor and against the rich. Dinka, his friend, told J that Naxals would kill all rich people of the town and distribute their wealth among the poor. J was thrilled; at least Barda would get some wealth to run their household. J had a secret wish, he did not tell anybody. One day, he would sit on his own wooden chair, and study comfortably like Kabir, his classmate. If Barda got some money, he would surely buy a wooden chair exclusively for J. Barda loved him very much. The Naxals would surely give Barda some money after killing the rich people, because they were poor, J knew. Barda worked in the 'collectary' [Office of the District Collectorate (Magistrate)]; he was a copywriter there. After father became paralytic, the onus of looking after all brothers, sisters and the mother fell on Barda. Father was out of job for a long time, J heard. Chhorda and Fagun got jobs very recently. Now things might improve a bit. But the family had huge loans to repay, J heard elders discuss, due to the prolonged illness of father, and very expensive treatment of his multifarious diseases. If the Naxals gave some of the rich men's money to Barda, things would definitely improve.

Was Bishnu Pada Saha a rich man? J tried to remember. He had gone to his shop several times to bring essentials on credit. He was an old untidy person with white beard, and often enquired of J about his studies. J heard that he had big godowns to stockpile rice, pulse, sugar, wheat and many other essentials. J also had the chance to visit one such store-house. Once he had gone there with one of Saha's employees. He saw big sacks full of essential goods stacked all over the place. It was a dingy medium-sized room; and from there Saha's employees brought materials to the grocery shop when essential items went out of stock in the shop. Saha was known as a rich trader in their locality, and the Naxals killed him.

J knew that Naxals were those people who had written in Bengali "Chiner Neta, Amader Neta" (China's Leader is our Leader) all over the town. It appealed to J. The slogan was very catchy and a bit rhythmic too. Some slogans carried the picture of a flabby-cheeked person. J came to know his name, because it was written below the picture: Chenglei Yang. J did not like the picture, the man resembled Gopal-da, a vagabond in their locality. Dinka told J that some senior boys in their locality had become Naxals. J looked at them with awed reverence, with a little bit of jealousy, and felt an inexplicable chivalry within. These G'das and H'das would kill all rich people of the town and distribute their wealth among the poor. They were the modern Robin Hoods, J started to believe.

Barda was tense for another reason. Fagun had come to town on leave. He was now with the police, and the Naxals were targeting the police as their enemy. They were killing policemen all over the state. Barda told Fagun not to go outside the house alone. Fagun protested; it was his town, he grew up here, why would he not venture outside? The sisters also supported Fagun. Barda said it was bad time when old friends were turning into foes, and requested Fagun to pay heed to him. Fagun did not argue further, but he was also tense, J could feel. Why Naxals were against poor policemen, J wondered in his thoughts. Were poor policemen different from poor people? J knew that Chhorda and Fagun had to make and sell small paper packets to support their studies. Now that one of them had joined the police to support a poor family, he became the target of the Naxals? J thought Barda was tense for the wrong reason. Naxals were good people; they never killed anyone poor.

Amit-da, J knew, was a Naxal, and a hero in their locality. He stood first in the district (in the Science Stream) at the Higher Secondary Examination. The local club recently felicitated him. He was a hero to J for another reason. Dinka told J that Amitda joined the Naxals. J wanted to be close to Amitda, like all fans to their heroes. But J found Amitda very rude. He never talked to J, like other senior dadas in the club did. He was very harsh. The other day he slapped J on the face for wanting to continue a badminton practice beyond his allotted quota. J was shocked; tears rolled down his cheeks although he did not cry. Sonali-di came forward and put her soft, mother-like hands on J's shoulders. J felt good, although he expected Sonali to say something to Amit; but Sonali didn't.

Sonali-di was close to Amit-da, Dinka told J. Dinka once saw them in Amit's house. The house was empty. Dinka went for Amit. The door was half-closed. Dinka saw Amit holding Sonali from back. Sonali, Dinka saw, was lifting her Sari with one hand as Amit was pushing his front towards Sonali's back; and both were gasping. Dinka silently came out, but rushed to find J and narrate what he had seen. Dinka made J promise not to reveal this to anybody. J didn't. But he felt curious. What were they doing? Fighting? J failed to understand. He felt bad for Sonali. Could a beautiful lady win a physical fight against a man? Then why Sonali was fighting with Amit? Were they really close friends? But Dinka said they were close. In fact all the didis (senior girls) of the locality wanted to be close to Amit, he was so brilliant; and brilliant boys, Dinka told J, were huge favourites among girls. But brilliant boys were rare in the locality. J had decided that he would be brilliant, for not only to attract girls, but shatter Amitda's pride and rudeness as well.

J rushed home that afternoon to tell Barda that Amit had slapped him, but Barda had not come back from office.

He found only Chhordi in the house, as all others went out. In the evening no one stayed at home. J told Chhordi about the incident, but Chhordi only laughed and said, "Elders have the right to slap juniors. Besides..." Chhordi continued, "...Amit is so brilliant, he would not slap you for nothing". J felt a lump blocked inside his throat, he could not say anything; although he wanted to shout. The only thing he could do was come out of the house.

A gloomy evening greeted him outside. J walked slowly, the lump still inside. He found his friends Babu, Dinka, Kabir, Gundi and Utpal sitting on the green patch beside the asphalt road, near the club. They were engrossed in their evening 'adda' (informal talk). J joined the group, but remained silent. He could hear his friends debating over the result of a local cricket match. But their voices, J felt, were coming from a very distant, faraway place, as if they were not around, as if their voices were coming from the stars above in this dark and ugly evening. J looked up and found a few stars in the sky. Was father residing there? Or was he in the winds, floating as a spirit? Had the spirit of his father seen Amit slapping J? He must have seen it. Spirits could see everything. But why did not his father react? Why did he not slap Amit? Why did he not lift Amit from the ground to the winds? For the first time J felt he was demanding something from his father, from his dead father. He wished his dead father could be stronger than the paralytic, living father. Only a strong spirit could shatter Amit-da's pride for brilliance. J wished from the core of his heart that the spirit of his father must not be a paralytic crippled one. It should be as strong, as powerful, and as magical like any other spirit. Otherwise, the spirit could never punish Amit.

Brilliants might know early what the spirits were up to. Brilliants were not like ordinary men.

But God was very cruel and selfish. He had given the brilliants everything, - intelligence, intellect, rudeness, attention from girls, and the right to slap juniors! But he had not given the little ones anything. Only grown-ups could be brilliant, not the little ones. J decided he would be brilliant, but he would never slap children. He would allow all children to continue badminton practice; he would not be harsh, he would be very polite and affectionate to the little ones.

Kabir's mother came to call him home, and the group dismantled. J was now feeling better. The idea of a continued badminton practice for all children gave him fresh breath. The stubborn lump finally started to go down his throat as J began walking for home. When J was nearing home, Sonali-di appeared from nowhere, and lifted J.

"Were you hurt? Amit always behaved like that, very ill-tempered", Sonali consoled J.

J felt better in the warmth of Sonali's arms.

"But Amit is not bad you know, he is after all very brilliant", pleaded Sonali, "I will take you home after a few rounds; are you comfortable?"

J nodded; he was indeed feeling very well. A gentle breeze started blowing and J could smell the fragrance of a very well-known odour. Was it from the 'Batabi' flowers, or from Sonalidi's gentle touch? J was not sure. But the scent was very much known, a very close and dear one. Sonalidi kissed J like a mother, "You are such a lovely child". J could not remember when his own mother or elder sisters kissed him. That was why Sonalidi was so different, so special, and so loved by J.

"Is Amit-da a Naxal"? J suddenly asked Sonalidi. Sonali stood for a while, looked vacantly at J's eyes and then brought him down slowly to the ground. J felt uncomfortable.

"Who told you"?

J was going to say Dinka's name, but remained silent.

"Amit thinks about the poor people, he thinks for the country", said Sonali.

"Don't ever say this to anybody", Sonali continued, "the Police are after the Naxals…" She resumed after a pause, "other political parties are also trying to finish them. But the Naxals will change our society; they will change the world for better. Everyone will get food and shelter, you, me, everybody in this country".

They stopped walking. The conviction in Sonali-di's voice attracted J as he watched Sonalidi continue, "Amit is against this inequality, rich men get everything, poor get nothing; this must stop. Amit says this will stop. He is not bad. He has a dream, and those who dream are unpredictable".

"I also dream every night, I dream about a lovely garden full of blue flowers and golden fruits. I also dream about Doms eating navels", J replied.

Sonali burst into laughter. "You are so cute, so innocent… We all dream, but Amit's dreams are different. Brilliant people can dream differently; they are not like you and me… However don't ever say this to anybody; Amit would be very angry if he hears all these".

J decided that he would not tell this ever to anybody, not because of Amitda's anger, but because of Sonalidi's affection. They again started walking. Encouraged by Sonalidi's talks, J said, "What is Chiner Neta, Amader Neta? Who is Chenglei Yang?"

"Oh, you must have read the graffiti", replied Sonalidi, "I also don't know. All I know is that there is a country called Chin" (China).

"That I also know", declared J proudly, "and Barda said they defeated us in a war".

"War!" Sonali wondered, "but when did it take place?" J kept silent; he did not know. Sonali also did not say anything for a while; she appeared to be thoughtful to J.

"Yes, yes I can remember now... then I was in the Fourth Grade", Sonali broke her silence, "let me calculate... that was seven years ago...yes that was in the year... yes, I can now remember... no light, deserted roads, sounds of aeroplanes... father said it was a war".

"I like wars, so exciting, so fascinating, like a game; but Barda says wars are not good", J told in a sinking voice.

"Wars are not good, so many people die, so many become homeless", Sonali said like a prophet.

"Barda said India was defeated, and Chin won. Mehra was very upset", J also matched the prophet in wisdom.

"Mehra? Who was Mehra?" Sonali wondered.

"Our Prime Minister", J replied like a Headmaster.

"Don't talk rubbish", Sonali retorted, "Priti Gautam is our Prime Minister. She is like an angel; so good-looking, can beat any film star in her looks".

J got confused. Barda said Banwari Lal Mehra was the Prime Minister, then why this angel-lady? Barda could never be wrong; Sonalidi did not know the truth. Mehra was the Prime Minister. Prime Ministers were big people, very powerful, very rich, and always busy. They travelled in aeroplanes, in motor cars, policemen saluted them. Could a big policeman with a big moustache salute a lady? Sonalidi must be wrong. J knew for certain, Mehra was the Prime Minister.

But how does one become a Prime Minister? Can J become a Prime Minister when he grows up? He wants to be a Prime Minister because he can travel in aeroplanes, if he becomes the Prime Minister.

"How can one become a Prime Minister, Sonalidi?" J asked.

"Ladies are selected on the basis of their beauty, men on the basis of strength. Look at Priti Gautam, she is so beautiful", Sonali said with confidence.

J instantly decided he would be strong. But who is Priti? Is she really the Prime Minister? J will ask Barda. Only he can clear J's confusions.

"You said Chin defeated us in the war?" Sonali asked.

"Yes Barda told me so", J replied.

"Is that true", Sonali asked again.

"Barda can never be wrong", J said with pride.

"Yes that is true, Barda is so wise, he can't be wrong", Sonali agreed.

"Chin is great, that's why Naxals prefer Chin. Look they defeated us in the war", Sonali continued.

"But in a war the opposing side is your enemy", the Headmaster in J retorted, "Why would you prefer an enemy?" Now Sonali got confused. After a pause she said in a low voice, "I will ask Amit. He is a Naxal, but don't you ever say this to anybody. He is very good, he is so brilliant. Brilliants are becoming Naxals now-a-days, you know".

*　　*　　*

Back home J found the familiar late evening scene, -
Fulda, Bhai, and Pari seated on the floor for studying around
a kerosene lantern. Chhordi was in the kitchen, preparing
Roti for dinner under a small kerosene lamp. An enamel
wok was on the oven; a vegetable curry was boiling inside,
J had realized from the familiar smell. Mother and Anjali
were not yet back. They would come late. Mother visited
different houses in the locality for juicy gossip, and Anjali,
J knew, was with her friends talking about 'cruel and
treacherous' boy-friends. Barda must be in Sitaram-da's
grocery, a favourite place for *adda* to all of Barda's friends.

These friends are peculiar, they belong to all professions
and age groups; - people from almost every corner of India,
who have settled in this town. There is among others in the
group, Mr. Saha, the local politician, who has contested the
Municipal elections and lost. His family is originally from
Bihar. There is Mr. Sahoo, bright-complexioned, diminutive
with a bald head, originally from Orissa, the mathematics
teacher in a local Hindi medium primary school. Sitaram,
the grocer, is originally from Uttar Pradesh. He is glad to
have the *adda* in his shop every evening. In fact, he prefers
adda more than his business, which is steadily declining.
Barda, the local copywriter, is another member of the group,
along with Mr. Swamy, the Tamil Christian who speaks
fluent Bengali. Mr. Swamy's forefathers, Barda told, had
come to Bengal and somehow settled in this town. Presently,
Mr. Swamy is the Headmaster of a Bengali medium school
which he himself established. J studies in Grade Three in
this school.

In fact J's admission process to the school was completed
in Sitaram's shop. That was four years ago, J could distinctly
remember. He went to the grocery with Barda. It was a

winter evening, and Barda's friends, J saw after reaching the shop, were having hot tea in earthen pots. Barda casually took J to the grocery, like fathers sometimes carried their children outside. Sitaram gave J two candies from a big glass-jar. Mr. Swamy enquired from Barda about J's age. Barda said J was three years old. Mr. Swamy then asked J whether he knew any poem. J enthusiastically said "Yes". Mr. Swamy asked him to recite. J promptly stood up, and started reciting in clear Bengali:

> Tal Gachh ak paye dariye
> Sab gachh chhariye
> Uki mare akashe
> Mone saadh phure jai
> Akebare ure jai
> Kotha pabe dana se!
>
> [The palm tree, standing on a single leg
> Above all trees
> Peeps at the sky
> Aspires to pierce the blue
> And fly forever
> From where shall it get wings!]

All of Barda's friends clapped and applauded J for a good recital. J instantly felt proud and happy. It was a famous poem written mainly for children by Rabindra Nath Tagore, Bengal's most respected poet. J learned it from Chhordi, and memorized it.

Mr.Swamy asked Barda whether he was thinking about J's schooling. Barda said, "not seriously". Mr. Swamy told Barda to send J to his school from the next morning. Barda was a bit confused, but his other friends enthusiastically urged Barda to send J to school. J recited so well, they opined, he was ready for school, and must be sent to school. J was very excited; he came home flying, like the palm tree in Tagore's poem.

That evening Barda announced in front of everybody that J would join Mr. Swamy's school.

"How come?" enquired Mother.

Barda said proudly, "he impressed Mr. Swamy at Sitaram's grocery".

"At Sitaram's grocery?" Mother was truly astonished. "What the grocery has to do with a school?"

"Mr. Swamy comes to the shop regularly", said a jubilant Barda.

"Who is Mr. Swamy?" asked Mother.

Now Fulda said, "you illiterate lady, Mr. Swamy is the Headmaster of the school".

Anjali suddenly said with all wisdom in her voice, "I know him, he is a Madrasee Christian. His only motto is to convert Hindu boys and girls to Christianity. That is why he has opened this school. He is a bad guy".

Now Mother shouted loudly at Barda, "who told you to take my child to that bad guy?"

Barda said softly that Mr. Swamy was a perfect gentleman, the best he had seen around, and his only mission was to educate poor children.

Mother started yelling, "Oh, my child would also be converted! Stop him O Rama, stop him O Krishna, stop him O Shiva, from going to school". Rama, Krishna and Shiva, any child like J knew, were all Hindu Gods.

J stood silently, bewildered, in front of the unfolding drama.

Now Barda started shouting at mother, "why you never thought about sending him to school? That's your duty".

Mother's yelling became louder, "if only his father was alive! He would have done everything for J, giving no scope to you, the rustic, to shout at his mother".

Barda retorted angrily, "phooh father, the paralytic for the last few years!"

Now Chhordi started crying, and intervened, "stop, all of you, please stop. If you don't want to respect your father, don't. But please think that he might be around, and he could hear you shouting. His spirit would be sad and ashamed; tears would come out from his eyes, and roll down his cheeks. He could not talk for some years before his death". Chhordi's voice had something that brought senses back. An eerie silence descended. Nobody talked much at dinner that night.

In the morning Chhordi prepared J for school, while mother watched silently in disapproval. Nobody protested or encouraged; a long winter night might have given enough wisdom to everybody. Barda took an excited J in his bicycle to the school. Mr. Swamy thanked Barda for getting J to school. When Barda left, J started crying; he felt all alone in the midst of strangers. The strangers looked like Satans, boys in black shorts and girls in black skirts, with white shirts for both. The school uniform appeared horrifying to J. He decided to run away, but found Mr. Swamy by his side. He took a sobbing J to a class room. It was a small room with a tiny window. Around twenty boys and girls sat on a cemented floor looking at the blackboard hanging from a pale wall. J saw a lady drawing a round-shaped thing on the blackboard. When Mr. Swamy appeared at the door with J, the lady stopped drawing, and looked back. Mr. Swamy said,

"One more child for you Madam". The lady non-chalantly told J, "Come in and sit down… at the rear end, near the window". J went in and sat down in between a boy and a girl as they made room for J. He was the only child without a school uniform. Earlier Barda told the Headmaster that he would get J the uniform within a week. The Headmaster agreed.

Was this what people called a school? No playground, a dilapidated house with dingy rooms full of dust and cramped walls? J thought school was all fun and play; but here five rows of satans were seated grimly on the cemented floor, all looking at him, as if he had come from another planet. The teacher was engaged in her drawing on the blackboard. When she was turning around occasionally, the students were paying attention to her; otherwise they remained boringly silent and stupidly seated. The school frustrated J on the very first day.

Suddenly he could feel a strange sensation inside his pant. Something was creeping on his thigh. Was it a scorpion? Utpal told J that scorpions were very poisonous. It could even be a small snake. Last month a very small black snake had entered their kitchen. It was a Sunday. Chhordi noticed it first. She thought it was a scorpion, but later Barda told it was a snake, a baby snake, and Barda killed it. Snakes should not be kept alive, they were very poisonous, everybody in the locality used to say. Barda smashed the baby snake with a brick and burned the little rope-like body in the backyard. Nitai Jethu (uncle), the elderly neighbour told Barda to remain alert. The baby snake's mother could take revenge. The entire household spent the week in fear. Had the mother sent another baby to take revenge on J now? J jumped up in fear and started screaming.

"What happened?" The teacher turned back, startled

"A snake inside", said J

"Inside, where, inside the room"? The teacher shot back

Now all the students got panicky. They jumped up. Some front-row students ran towards the door; one girl fell over another; there was a big stampede inside the classroom. Now the teacher yelled at the students, "Sit down, all of you, where is the snake? Who has seen it?" The students huddled around the teacher, panic in their eyes.

"Where is the snake"? The teacher now faced J and asked him. J stood bewildered amidst all the pandemonium

"WHERE IS THE SNAKE?" repeated the teacher emphatically as her eyes were scanning the room.

"Inside my pant", J replied like a machine, hearts stopped in fear.

"Inside your pant?" the teacher retorted with wonder.

The whole class felt curious.

"Open it immediately", the teacher ordered

J stood still, bewildered, unable to carry out the order. Now a courageous boy suddenly pulled down the elastic-waist pant as J stood half-naked in front of the class. A little cockroach, also bewildered in this atmosphere, could be seen above J's little penis. The class burst into laughter. To be sure, the teacher ordered the boy who pulled down J's pant, to search it thoroughly for the snake. Nothing could be found. The laughter became louder as those who ran out in fear came back, this time for fun. Only J, the half- naked human soul was crying amid the jeering laughter of the Satans. J decided that he would not come back to the satanic school again.

* * *

Another storm scorched their home that evening. Late evenings were times for informal family chats as everybody came back from their respective 'places'; - mother from her para rounds, sisters from their friends' places, J from local club, Barda from 'office', Bhai from the other para. Only Fulda and Chhordi used to stay at home.

"I knew the school was very bad, filthy and dirty and they didn't look after the children properly", mother said after hearing J's first day incident in the school from Chhordi.

"All these schools are actually made by opportunist people for more grants from the government", Anjali declared with usual wisdom.

"They take advantage of poverty. A lot of poor children are forcibly packed inside small rooms. More the number of students more is the amount of grant for the school. These schools are mushrooming, not to impart education but to amass wealth" she continued churning her wisdom.

"That's why she has stopped going to school", Fulda bantered.

Anjali, J knew, failed twice in her eighth grade.

Now Anjali retorted angrily, "You half -blind, you ridicule me! That's why God has made you half- blind".

Fulda had problems with his eyes, he could not see properly, but he liked to study a lot.

Now mother shot back, "How dare you call my son half blind? You illiterate stupid goat!"

"Eeeh here shouts the pundit! You ignorant, how dare you shout? You have never gone to any school in your entire life-time and now addressing me as an illiterate!" Anjali retorted.

"You fool, shouting at your own mother? You rascal, I may be illiterate, but all my sons are genius", mother said.

"Sons, sons and sons; you are always boasting about sons and neglecting daughters. That's why daughters don't get proper food and schooling, that's why they are bad at studies", replied Anjali.

"Yes, Anjali is right", joined Pari. "Hell with this biased mother, she neglects all her daughters".

"Stop you brat, otherwise I shall teach you a lesson". Mother took a broom in her hand.

"Come, beat me, that's the only thing you know, beating daughters and pampering sons. Oh God, don't you ever give a mother like this even to an enemy!" Pari started crying loudly.

Chhordi now entered the scene and yelled at mother, "I can't cook everyday for this huge family. That's not my job. That's the job and concern of a mother. She should think about feeding her children. Cook for your sons, if you love them so much. Don't you ever order me to cook for the entire family".

"Yes, yes, I will cook for them only, for my sons only and not for all of you, you ugly ducklings!" mother jeered at Chhordi.

"Oh God, see what a mother we have got, she calls her daughters ugly", Pari yelled.

"Yes, yes I am not scared to say the truth". Mother went on. "Have you ever watched yourself in the mirror? You look just like witches", mother shot back.

J knew that witches looked horrible. They had dark complexions with big teeth and sharp long nails. Now Chhordi started crying, "Look God, a mother is calling her own daughters witches! Oh Lord what a mother you have bestowed on us".

"A witch must be called a witch; God loves those who tell the truth", mother ridiculed.

"Something is burning in the oven", Barda screamed.

Mother rushed to the kitchen but came back shortly. "Look the rice is burning there but the witches are shouting here", she told with anger

"Eeeeh! the rice is burning in the kitchen, but look at our mother; she has come rushing back from the kitchen to continue the squabble", grinned Anjali.

"Am I an idiot like you?" Mother shouted at the top of her voice. "I have put down the rice pot from the oven".

"Without straining the starch", Pari retorted, "that rice would be like a starchy rice cake with a fantastic burnt aroma".

Now mother was caught unaware. She again rushed back to the kitchen.

"So fond of quarrelling that she often forgets everything", Barda said loudly.

"Oh Lord, for those I steal, (they) call me a thief!" mother shouted from the kitchen. "I always speak in support of my sons, but they only insult me, Oh Lord, have justice on me", she said.

"Who told you to speak for your sons and put the entire household on fire?" Fulda retorted.

Now mother started crying and abusing her ill-luck. "Good boys are always selfish, they don't care about their mothers". Fulda was known as a good student in the locality.

"Your sons will carry you to heaven, your brriilliiaanntt sons", Anjali said loudly.

"Yes they will, who told you to interfere, stupid witch?" Mother shot back again.

*   *   *

J was trying to remember the issue upon which the storm began. It was his first-day incident at the school. But the actual issue was blown far away by the storm, although it was the main cause behind the storm. Some times J thought that his home was more like a big lunatic asylum. J learned from his friends that in a lunatic asylum mentally ill people lived and always shouted and jeered at each other. His household definitely resembled a lunatic asylum. But even then J loved this house very much although he did not know why. Perhaps because J lived in this house, ate, drank and slept here. It was in this house where he dreamed about the lovely garden, golden fruits, orange sky and the silvery river gently flowing through the green, - lovely green and scenic meadows. J now began to visualize some of his splendid dreams, amid all squabbles around. It took him away from the storm.

3

BLOODY CRICKET

Durga Puja is late this year. Puja time is the best part of the year. New clothes, new shoes, the feel-good fragrance in the air, and long holidays in school, make the Puja time really wonderful. The season is best suited for the festivities after long spell of nagging monsoon. The sky gets clear with milk-white clouds floating all over the turquoise-blue sky. The golden autumn-sun shines brightly. The aroma of shiuli (a flower that typifies autumn), the shiny dew drops on the grass and the swinging white 'Kash' flowers by the side of the Ganga, announce silently the arrival of Durga Puja in this part of the world. Each year Goddess Durga comes down to earth from the Kailash Parbat (Hills), the abode of Shiva and Durga along with her daughters Laxmi and Saraswati and sons Ganasha and Kartik. Laxmi is the Goddess of wealth, Saraswati is the Goddess of knowledge, Ganesha is the God of trade and business and Kartik is the God of tools and machines. Among this family of gods and goddesses Ganesha is the most attractive, with the head of an elephant and the body of a fat man. Ganesha has a big bulging belly and quite a huge weight, but every year he comes down to the earth sitting on a mouse! Lord Ganesha evokes tremendous curiosity in J.

Last year J wanted to know from his mother why Lord Ganesha had the head of an elephant. But his mother was unsure. J asked Dinka and he told that once Ganesha had killed an elephant and wore its head. This answer did not sound convincing to J; so he asked Barda. But then Barda was in a hurry for his office and told J that he would tell the story later. But Barda forgot to tell the story about Ganesha after returning from office. J asked Sonalidi. She said that Ganesha could wear the mask of any animal at any time. J realized that Sonalidi too did not know the exact answer. He then asked Kabir, Utpal and many other para guys about the elephant-head of Ganesha. Now the para boys started to make fun of J and began to call him 'Ganesha'. Finally J relented. But each year during Durga Puja, Lord Ganesha evoked the same curiousity. Now J had stopped asking anyone about Ganesha, not even Barda. He realized that Barda was too preoccupied with his own 'business' of running and guiding the 'lunatic asylum' and attending his office. When Barda got free-time, he used to go to Sitaram's shop and spend the entire evening there. Where was the time to answer J about Ganesha's head!

*   *   *

But Durga Puja is different. After all it is a time for unbound joy and happiness. The joy starts exactly a week before the four grand days of the Puja, with the 'Mahalaya', when people start welcoming the Goddess to earth. On the day of Mahalaya the elders go to the river Ganga to offer pujas and pray for their forefathers. In the early morning of the 'Mahalaya', All India Radio airs a special programme narrating the story of 'Mahishasurmardini' (the killer of demon). A radio artiste with a nasal voice unfolds the story of how Goddess Durga killed the powerful demon Mahishasur and all his associates. When demonic forces unleash terror, all noble powers unite, becoming one divine force called Shakti or Durga, and that force is worshipped by the people during Durga Puja. The narration of the artist is interspersed with songs, - solo and chorus, and the programme continues for an hour or so. The kids, the elders, men and women of the locality wake up early in the morning and listen to the radio programme religiously. J's three sisters, mother, Bhai, Fulda, Barda, all listen to the programme with rapt attention. Chhordi says that it is always virtuous to listen to this programme of 'Mahalaya' as it relates the tale of goddess Durga's glorious victory and her visit to her paternal home on Earth. On every 'Mahalaya' morning the grand old 'Murphy' radio in J's house is brought down from the top of the broken almirah and cleaned, because of the lurking fear that it may stop in the middle of the programme. But surprisingly, it never stopped during this programme in the last few years. Chhordi believes that Mother Durga's good wishes prevented the Radio from going off the air during the programme. Unlike their biological mother, Mother Durga is very kind, gracious and of course enormously powerful, thinks Chhordi.

But the 'Mahalaya' morning is different to J and his friends for another reason. Season's first cricket game is introduced every year on the 'Mahalaya' morning. It is highly exciting to play cricket in the semi dark junction of late night and mystique early autumn morning, when the dew drops tenderly clean the green grass, when the sweet fragrance of fresh 'shiuli' flower fills the air. The team that reaches the ground first gets the best pitch and the late-comers remain satisfied only with the uneven bumpy stone-topped pitch. J could embarrassingly remember how he woke up at 2 a.m. a couple of years ago thinking that his friends had called him to accompany them to the ground. He had hurriedly woken up to join his friends, but only heard his mother snoring. The boring and monotonous sound brought him back to senses. It was just a dream. Chhordi whispered from one corner of the room, 'Don't get up, it is very dark outside', and J went to sleep again.

But this year J's team is fully equipped with three stumps, a bat and two old tennis balls, popularly known as 'cambis' balls among boys. One of the two balls had lost its soft skin and become 'baldy'. Such balls are in great demand among the 'clever' bowlers, because they spin menacingly. Pieces of red bricks will be stacked one over the other to make stumps at the bowler's end. Such bricks had already been stolen from the site of a house under construction in the locality. So the boys this year are fully equipped with all cricketing gears. Last year they could manage only two stumps for the batsman's end and one brick for the bowler's end, and they were late to reach the ground as well. Cricket had to be played on a bumpy pitch last year and there was hardly any joy.

This year is totally different. The boys are well equipped. They have already taken the firm resolution of waking up early in the morning to grab the best 'pitch'. Durga Puja is late this year. There is already a chill in the air. J and his friends are eagerly waiting to play the cricket match on a chilly and mysterious morning of late autumn.

Even three days ago there was an uncertainty about this year's plan for cricket. The cricket bat used last year had broken and there was hardly any hope of getting a new one. J had watched rich boys of other localities go to shops selling sports goods, and buy new cricket bats. But J and his friends could not afford to buy new bats. They always depended on the local carpenters who used to curve out bats from pieces of wood that were procured by J or any one of his friends. This year they could not manage a single piece of wood even a month ago. But Goddess Durga finally had mercy on them, and come as a saviour. Utpal's father, comparatively well off among all others in the para, planned to make a new wooden almirah for his house before the Puja. Timber arrived at Utpal's house. Carpenters started the work there. When J and his friends were informed about this, they were struck by the idea. They knew that Raghu-da, the master carpenter working at Utpal's house was soft on young boys. So J and his friends decided to request Raghuda to make a bat for them. 'But father would be very angry', Utpal told his friends. Last night Utpal heard his parents talking about the escalating price of timber. Niladri assured Utpal that Raghuda would not tell Utpal's father. But Utpal was not sure as he knew that Raghuda was a trusted man of his father. When Kabir suggested approaching Raghuda with their idea, Utpal became nervous. He thought that if his father came to know about the grand strategy, he would be extremely angry and would beat him severely with a solid piece of wood. Dinka suggested that for the sake of cricket as well as for the sake of his friends, Utpal should take the risk. Utpal protested and said that he would invite Dinka to bear the brunt of his father's anger and to get the beating. Dinka took up the challenge and said that he was ready to be thrashed for the sake of cricket; - he actually had the courage. Utpal did not like Dinka's acceptance of the challenge, as well as his body language. He angrily retorted, 'Do you call me a coward?'

"Yes, you are. You are also selfish as well. You don't want to give us a bat made from only a piece of your father's stock of woods", replied an angry Dinka. Gundi supported Dinka instantly.

A furious Utpal protested, "Look, it was me who informed you about the carpenters' work at my house. Otherwise you wouldn't have known about it at all. And now you are blaming me and calling me coward…selfish…"

Kabir came to Utpal's support and said "Yes, Utpal had a good intention. Nobody can deny that"

"You always support him, the stooge", Gundi shouted back

"What? You call me a stooge? You brainless idiot, failed in Grade Six twice", Kabir was fuming.

Now the boys were clearly divided into two camps. But Gundi did not say anything. He appeared morose as he kept quiet. J could realize what had hurt Gundi. Kabir had hit Gundi where it pained most. Everybody knew that Gundi was always ashamed about his performance in examinations.

But the greatest casualty was the cricket bat. Niladri tried to save the situation desperately, "We are perhaps the greatest fools on earth. The bat is nowhere but we are fighting among ourselves." Aziz, Barun and J supported Niladri.

"We have no bat this year and the Mahalaya is only twenty days away", said Aziz in a pensive mood

"I am not interested", said Utpal

"I am not interested either", Kabir told philosophically

"We all are interested" Barun retorted in a commanding tone, "We all are interested because the prestige of the para is involved"

Now everybody including the mellowed Gundi became curious.

"Prestige of the para?" asked Aziz

"Yes, prestige of the locality will go down the drain if cricket is not introduced on the Mahalaya morning. Boys of other localities would jeer at us. They'll mock and taunt us to tears. Will you accept it if they call us lazy idiots?" said Barun

"He's right. Why haven't we thought in this line earlier?", J wondered out loud

"We can do one thing", Niladri joined, "We can meet Raghuda at his residence on Sunday morning. He does not go to work on Sundays. We all should go to his place except Utpal. If Utpal does not go his father would not suspect anything"

"Rubbish!", Utpal broke his silence, "Father is no fool not to realize that I have informed all of you. I'll also go. I don't care what happens tomorrow. Cricket must be played on the Mahalaya morning"

*   *   *

Next Sunday, the boys went up to Raghuda's house. Raghuda listened to their demand patiently. But he expressed his helplessness in this matter. The boys got utterly frustrated and hopeless.

A dejected Niladri said, "Raghuda, the prestige of the para is at stake. You also live in the same locality"

"Yes, that is true", Raghuda replied, "But for me, my employer's prestige is much more important"

Pointing towards Utpal Raghuda said, "His father is such a gentleman, always helping poor men like us. I can't cheat on him."

"Please do something, Raghuda", pleaded Dinka in a last-ditch effort, "Mahalaya is round the corner"

"Sorry boys, this time I can't help you" replied Raghu in a serious tone

The boys lost their last hope and set out to return to the para club.

"I always thought that Raghuda cooperated with the young. Now it seems, I was so wrong", said a dejected Aziz

"He pretends to be kind but he is a villain" retorted Barun, visibly agitated

"We should not have gone to his place. It was a sheer wastage of time" murmured Barun

Now Gundi said, "Can you hear? Raghuda is calling us"

The boys looked back. Raghu was indeed calling them. "No use going back, he will tell all nonsense to appease us", burst out Kabir!

"Yes we should not go", said Dinka.

"But we can hear him at least", pleaded Utpal who was not very angry with Raghu, because Raghu had praised his father in front of all his friends.

"Then do one thing. You and J go back to Raghuda. We are waiting here", said Kabir.

Utpal and J went back. Raghu said, "I had forgotten one thing. I have some spare pieces of wood, actually left-over from last month's work at Harenbabu's place. They were handed over to me by Harenbabu after I completed his work. I think I can make a bat out of that stock". Utpal had an instant reaction. He jumped in the air with joy, embraced and hugged Raghuda. Other boys who were watching them from a distance ran speedily towards Raghuda. Gundi, tall and strong, lifted the diminutive Raghu and tossed him in the air. "Leave me, I have other work". Raghu said, "Let me finish the bat first and then you celebrate"

"We know you would do a good job", said Aziz, "We know you are a great carpenter, the best in town"

"It will take some time", replied Raghu, "As you know, I have other work. After all I'll have to satisfy my customers first, I get paid for that. So I will work for the bat in my spare time".

"Raghuda, please finish it at least seven days before the Mahalaya" requested Barun

"I will try, but I cannot promise", Raghu said

"No, not seven days Raghuda, finish it at least three days before", requested J

"I said I'll try" replied Raghu, "but I can't promise"

Finally the bat came to their possession only four days before the Mahalaya. On his way back from work Raghu came to the club and handed it over to the boys. The bat was shinning with dark wooden polish

"Oh, you also polished it Raghuda!", exclaimed Niladri with joy, "it looks so nice and solid". "Bring a cambis ball", Aziz said, "I will check the bat and its level of endurance"

"Stop you stupid goat", ordered a commanding Kabir, "It will only be used on the Mahalaya morning"

All others supported Kabir. A brand new bat can never be used before the Mahalaya.

"I'll take the bat with me to my house and ask Bardi (eldest sister) to wrap it with a piece of cloth", said Niladri

"Yes that sounds better", opined Gundi, "Otherwise it might gather dust in this small and dingy clubroom". Everyone knows that Niladri is highly capable of keeping cricketing gears with utmost care. He is a specialist in this job.

Tomorrow is Mahalaya and all the boys are bubbling with joy. This year they will show the boys of 'Ghosh Para', 'Ukil Para' and 'Shasan Para' that they can also manage to be well equipped for a cricket match. Last year the boys of other localities had laughed at them when they started playing with only two stumps. This year they will be able to display boastfully all their cricketing gears. J knows that all his friends will spend a sleepless night. At 4 a.m. in the morning, Dinka will call him in his loud voice. Or it may be Aziz or Gundi, who knows! But generally Dinka calls him every year. They assemble in the club ground first, and then proceed to the big ground as a team. They were late last year. It must not be repeated this year, thought J.

Dinner will be served early at J's house this evening. Usually they take dinner late. But this evening is different, because tomorrow is 'Mahalaya'. Everybody will get up very early. Chhordi has been repeatedly requesting Barda for the last seven days to take the 'Murphy' radio to the mechanic's shop for repair. But Barda could not manage time to carry the radio to the repairing shop. They had a huge quarrel over it as usual. Finally Chhordi told Barda, like she did every year, that Goddess Durga would spoil all the evil plans of Barda to deprive Chhordi from listening to the holy Mahalaya programme aired by All India Radio. She wiped the radio clean with a piece of cloth and placed it on a shaky wooden table. She also covered it with a milk white lacy cloth. Every year it is placed on the same place so that its sound is audible to everybody at home. While wiping away the dust from the radio, Chhordi prayed to the Goddess and murmured, "Look Maa Durga, don't spare anybody who doesn't want you, who does not love you and your disciples. Don't spare the Satans". Barda only smiled.

J went to bed early this evening, fully satisfied that they were equipped with all the cricketing gears this year. He started thinking about his square drives and pulls. He saw himself diving forward to take a splendid catch. He was after all known as a brilliant fielder. Suddenly he heard his friends, - Dinka, Utpal and others, - were calling him loudly. Ah, the night had actually passed in his dreams and the cherished morning arrived! "But what a shame", thought J. He had been sleeping for so long! He was so callous! He could not wake up early. Screams of boys mellowed down gradually. J thought that his friends who had come to call him, left for the ground leaving behind a sleeping J. Now he shouted, "Wait, I am coming. Wait. Don't go away; Dinka I am coming"

"Oh my God, the same old story! J why do you shout at this wee hour of night. Stop it my Captain, it's only 1.30 a.m. Try to sleep. My sleep is gone anyway", said a dejected Pari. Bhai's laughter could be heard in darkness.

"He must be dreaming, don't laugh at him", Chhordi said.

"Give him a glass of water", Barda said, "He needs it"

Everyone woke up at J's shrieks. J back to his senses now, felt utterly ashamed. He grasped the pillow and hid his face in it.

"Go to sleep everybody", Barda ordered, "all you people can manage is only three hours sleep from now".

*   *   *

Anjali, known as the morning bird in the family, woke J up and informed that it was 4.15 a.m. J jumped out of his bed and went to the washroom. It was still dark outside and a bit chilly too. Did Dinka call him? J inquired. Anjali said, "I don't know. I heard nothing". She gave two pieces of 'roti' and some 'gur' to J. He ate them hurriedly and swallowed a glass of water. Now both could hear Dinka's voice, "J are you ready, come quickly". J rushed to the door, opened the bolt and went out. "Oh my God, such a devoted cricketer, if this devotion could be used in studies..." ridiculed Anjali. But J had no time to argue. The long-awaited Mahalaya morning has finally arrived.

Every one reached their small club ground except Barun. "As usual late, really Barun is incorrigible", said Kabir. "Yes for his late arrival we lost the best pitch last year", shouted an angry Niladri who brought all the cricketing gears from his house with utmost care. He carried the bat wrapped up in an old sari. Dinka and J started 'catch practice' with a cambis ball, as did Utpal and Gundi with an old 'baldy' cambis ball. Barun was nowhere to be seen, he lived far off; and the boys were getting late.

"We can't wait any longer", said an infuriated Kabir, "The pitch will be occupied"

"But Barun has not yet arrived, I think we should wait for him for some more time", Niladri argued

"Yes we should, we can't afford to leave him; he is such a good fielder", said Aziz

"But we'll be late, Tapas and his gang will capture the best pitch", Kabir was referring to the Ghosh para boys.

"We can do one thing", suggested Gundi, "some of us can proceed to occupy the best pitch and the rest can wait for Barun"

"That is a good idea", replied Kabir, "Gunndi and I shall wait for Barun and all others will proceed to the ground"

They ran for the big ground a kilometer away from the club; - Dinka, J, Aziz, Niladri and others. Everyone had some cricketing gear in his hand, - either a stump, or a ball, or a brick. Niladri was carrying the precious new bat.

When they were approaching the big ground from the northern side they saw another gang of boys from the opposite end. Whether they were the Ghosh para boys or the Shasan para, one could not make out from a distance in this semi-dark condition. But those boys were running as well, to grab the best pitch. Suddenly Niladri surged forward, followed by Utpal who was carrying a stump. They were the best runners in the team. Two boys from the opposite side also increased their speed. Now it was distinctly visible that they were the 'Shasan para' boys. Soon both the groups reached the best pitch at the same time. Utpal planted the stump at one end of the pitch as did Mawna, the Shasan para guy at the other end, to establish 'first' arrival. Severe bickering started, as both claimed that they had reached first. Soon it turned into an open fight. J got a big punch on his jaw. It was Pala of Shasan para who hit J. J sat on the ground in tremendous pain, while Pala was confronted by others of J's gang. It was free for all. Niladri punched Gaba in the face. The scuffle escalated amid free exchange of blows. Suddenly someone from the opposite gang hit Niladri with a stump. Niladri fell on the ground. Blood was oozing out of his head and he was writhing in extreme pain. His face and his cream-coloured shirt were smeared with blood. It was a horrifying sight. The Shasan para boys stared at Niladri for a while, whispered among them, and had disappeared within seconds as Niladri remained unconscious in a pool of blood. Aziz started crying as he could not bear this gruesome sight. Gundi picked up a handful of grass, smacked them on Niladri's wound. Gundi's hand was full of blood as well. Now Kabir tore off the cover of their new bat and pressed it hard on Niladri's head. The white cloth soon turned red.

"Let's call a rickshaw and take him to the Hospital", Utpal suggested.

But no rickshaw could be seen around. It was very early in the morning and a holiday as well. Rickshaw pullers hardly got out in this wee hour of the morning. Niladri somehow gained his consciousness and the first thing he said was 'don't inform anybody at my home'. He continued in a feeble voice, 'Father would be very angry'.

"Don't worry, we will not inform", assured Kabir, "but you must not talk in this condition"

"I will go to my house and steal my family's bicycle and carry Niladri to the Hospital", said Dinka.

"That's a good idea, but your mother is too alert and she has very sharp ears", warned Kabir.

"Don't worry; she will be engrossed listening to the Mahalaya programme on radio. I will climb the boundary wall silently, open the front door and bring out the bi-cycle, none will notice", said an excited Dinka

"But who will shut the door behind you"? asked Kabir

"I will do the needful. I will accompany Dinka", said Aziz, "I will shut the door after Dinka leaves with the biycle, and will come out crossing the boundary wall again"

'Ok', replied Kabir.

"Whatever you want to do, do it quickly" moaned Niladri, "I can't bear the pain any longer"

"Niladri, please remain silent, you are not well", ordered Kabir.

Shibu tore off the remaining portion of the bat-cover and pressed it on Niladri's head, as Dinka and Aziz ran for the bicycle. J noticed that a police jeep was approaching the ground. At first the boys got a little scary, but they were helpless and watched the jeep coming towards them and stopping nearby. Two men with Khaki police uniform jumped out of the jeep.

"What happened? Why is this boy bleeding?" one of the two inquired

"He was hit on his head by a Shasan para guy", complained Kabir

"Gang rivalry on this auspicious Mahalaya day!" mocked a policeman

"All for cricket, uncle" replied J innocently.

"Smart boy, very smart boy indeed! Now give him the cricket ball to swallow as medicine", the Policeman continued his rumbling.

"Stop Amar, the boy is bleeding profusely. We must take him to the hospital", remarked the other Policeman.

"You don't know these urchins Sir, they will never die", ridiculed Amar, the Policeman.

"Don't kill time Amar. The boy is bleeding profusely and his condition is not good, we must not delay", said the officer.

"Make him lie down on one side of the back seat, and some of you sit on the other side", the officer ordered the boys.

"I can walk", Niladri said as he started crawling towards the jeep. He managed to step into the jeep with some effort and lay on one of the rear seats. Kabir, Gundi and Utpal took their seats on the opposite side, as the two Policemen sat on the front. J heard Niladri pleading, "Don't inform my house Sir, father would be very angry".

"Then why do you fight?" asked the officer.

"They are like that sir, like animals", said Amar nonchalantly as the jeep sped off.

Aziz and J collected the cricketing gears. In a depressive mood they started walking towards their club. J felt some pain in his jaw. He thanked Ma Durga because he was at least better off than Niladri at this point of time

"I will not spare them", whispered an agitated Barun, "I will definitely teach those rowdies a lesson"

"Let Niladri recover first. Then we will think about revenge", J also whispered in a pensive mood.

It was no longer dark, people started coming out; one or two bicycles and rickshaws could be seen around. A gentle breeze blowing across carried the aroma of the 'Shiuli' flower. The horizon was waiting for the sun to rise. But J felt gloomy inside. Hurt and humiliated, J thought that only Maa Durga could erase this Mahalaya from their cricket history. Only Maa Durga could make Niladri his friend, bat again. He started praying to the Almighty Durga for an early recovery of Niladri.

4

MAGYAR POSTA

On an April evening, J could fondly remember that moment when the setting sun of the spring had painted the town orange. The trees, their leaves, the dusty winding road, the nearby little pond and the vast sky were all drenched in a flaming hue. This was the image of a universe J had dreamt of several times. J watched Barda from a distance returning home soaked in the orange colour of nature. The setting sun had cast an orange glow on Barda's bicycle too. Barda entered the house and told mother, who was getting ready for her evening stroll that 'Refugees' had flocked the town. Mother got startled, noticed J.

"Refugees again?" asked Mother, "But why?"

"Yes, Refugees again. This time they have taken shelter in our office corridor, outside our office room. It is very difficult to work in this condition. So I came back early", replied Barda.

"Oh God, Refugees again, has 47 reappeared?" mother replied anxiously and tensely. That was a rare sight for J. He had hardly seen mother worried.

"The situation in East Pakistan is not good. Pakistani soldiers had put Abdul Rahman behind the bars", Barda told mother.

"Who is Abdul Rahman?" asked mother.

"The supreme leader of the Freedom League, the party fighting for the rights of the Bengali-speaking people of East Pakistan", Barda replied. Now everybody got curious, Chhordi, Fulda, Mother and an ailing J. J was down with fever for several days. He was at home and watched Barda through the window pedaling his bicycle slowly, in the glowing canvas of orange.

"Yes, I have also seen them, people with wretched looks, begging from door to door", Fulda remarked.

"I thought they were the usual beggars", Chhordi said, "Yesterday, I gave one of them a roti"

"There are local beggars too", Barda said wisely, "but soon you will see their numbers swelling, then how many rotis can you manage to distribute? Refugees have also started begging, like local beggars".

"What happened in East Pakistan?" asked Mother impatiently.

"The Pakistani army had cracked down on the people of East Pakistan. Now the people want independence from West Pakistan", Barda informed.

"Who want independence?" shot back mother.

"The Bangla speaking people of East Pakistan", Barda replied.

"Hell with Pakistan and hell with independence! Independence in 1947 had made us Refugees. No need for more independence and many more refugees", mother said angrily. She was gasping.

"Calm down Ma, calm down. I remember everything although I was a child then, but calm down please. Rahman is fighting a tough battle for a greater cause. All the people of East Pakistan are behind him. He will create an independent Bangla", assured Barda.

"Oh, this dirty politics will once again suck the blood of the people. For God's sake no more politics", said Mother.

"Don't consider this as petty politics Ma", said Barda "This is all about the dream of a subjugated and tortured people of East Pakistan". Barda looked convincing to J, who remained a silent but intense listener.

"But who will take care of the Refugees, you?" asked mother. Mother came back to her actual self.

"I don't know, but I support Abdul Rahman and his freedom struggle", replied Barda.

J and his friends had also noticed women in tattered saris, and half-naked children carrying enamel bowls begging for food and cloth. But they also thought, like Chhordi, that these people were usual beggars. Now J remembered that these people could be seen everywhere – in the roads, markets, temples, mosques, offices, schools, - everywhere. The local beggars lived outside the town; but these new beggars were slowly crowding the town and living everywhere inside the town itself. J realized that these people were the 'Refugees'. But he could not understand why mother told that 1947 had made her a refugee too! Did his own mother look like those wretched women with children in their arms begging for survival, wondered J. J closed his eyes and tried to visualize his mother among the refugees but could not find her there. What happened in '47? J read in his History book that India achieved independence on 15th August, 1947. But why people had become refugees then,

J could not understand. Was independence so bad? But teachers in the school said that independence was a great event for India. Every year on 15th of August the national flag was hoisted in their school. A small ceremony was held on that day where students sang patriotic songs. Two years ago J was selected in the group which sang patriotic songs in front of many 'big' people. J felt very proud. Schools dissolved early after the ceremony on Independence Day and the whole day was there for fun and frolic, for play and 'adda'. Independence Day was always fantastic for J.

But now the word 'Refugee' has got entangled with independence, and his own mother is a refugee! J felt uncomfortable. Independence, for the first time in his life, has aroused a little pain inside. Who are the refugees? Why people become refugees? Why do they beg from door to door? Several questions haunted J's little mind. And on a Sunday morning, he tried to search for the answers from his 'man wisdom'.

Barda told him that people who got displaced from their 'homeland' were known as refugees: because these displaced persons had taken refuge in another land which was alien or unknown to them. The poor people who were found begging in the town now were actually the displaced people of East Pakistan. They had come to an alien land that was West Bengal in India crossing the border. But J had heard that borders were guarded by the 'military'! Barda smiled and said that East Pakistan and West Bengal had miles and miles of common border. It was not possible for the military to guard the entire border. These people came through the unguarded areas with great risk. If they were caught, they would be jailed. But why they got displaced from their homeland? "Because they are fighting for a separate country; they want to break away from Pakistan. And the military rulers in Pakistan do not want that, and they are trying forcibly to stop the movement for a separate state. They are torturing the leaders and people in general; and the people are fleeing their homeland, and taking refuge in West Bengal".

Barda explains everything so easily that J understands every bit. He is also reading the popular English newspaper regularly. Barda has recently told the newspaper vendor to give the 'English Paper' regularly. Barda thinks that they can afford a newspaper now, since Fagun and Chhorda are also earning. Moreover Fulda is studying the 'English Honours' course in the local college. The newspaper would be of immense help to him. Barda has also asked J to read the paper. J is now in standard Five. His command over the English language would be strengthened if he reads the paper from an early age, Barda has told J. Therefore J reads the paper regularly. Now-a-days the paper is full of news about the 'freedom struggle' in East Pakistan. But this newspaper does not print anything about 1947. Why people became refugees in 1947; why his own mother became a refugee in 1947? Was independence not a happy event then?

J asked mother one day: "Why you became a refugee in 1947"?

Mother curtly replied, "Jilqat, Pakistan, and the Foreign Rulers were all evils. They made us refugees". J did not understand. Who was Jilqat? J read in the history books that India and Pakistan became separate countries in 1947. But he never heard the name of Jilqat.

"Who was Jilqat", J asked mother.

"A devil, a satan; and Tarachand was no less; they all made us refugees. If Netaji had been alive things would have been different".

Everything became topsy-turvy for J. Tarachand is known as a great soul, J knows; he is also called the conscience of the nation, J also knows this. But here in the house, his own mother is calling Tarachand a 'satan', like Jilqat.

Mother was full of anger; her eyes were burning, J noticed, when she referred to Jilqat, Tarachand, Pakistan, Foreign Rulers…

"Tell me more Ma, what happened in 1947…" J asked.

"Oh those gory days… riots… huge fighting between Hindus and Muslims… people fled…thank God, we could also flee secretly… but you little boy, you super smart, what would you do knowing all details… you want to be a Politician? … Little children like you should not listen to those stories… stories of torture, humiliation, indignity, insult to humanity… Go play with your friends… you will know everything when you grow up…"

Mother went to the kitchen all of a sudden. The 'super smart' in J realized that mother was hiding something, as she was reliving those days of 1947

*   *   *

In Ojha sir's class J stood up and said "Tarachand was a satan, he divided the country and made people refugees". Ojha sir was referring to the freedom movement in the history class. The whole class, including the burly, clean-shaven, 'dhoti-kurta' clad Ojha was staring at J. But J continued as if he was possessed, "things would have been different had Netaji been alive".

"Sit down, my dear boy, sit down", Ojha said calmly. "Yes I know that people in Bengal love and respect Netaji... But calling Tarachand a satan is not appropriate... Anyway, how did you come to know about all these?"

J was going to tell that he came to know about these from his mother, but somehow resisted. His mother was illiterate after all! J remained silent.

"Somebody must have told you, or you must have read from somewhere... but these views are partial... not always correct... Tarachand wanted to avoid partition of India. He bled inside. But he could not resist the tide of time. Partition was a long history..." Ojha paused with a deep sigh.

"And Jilqat, he was also a devil", the super smart confidently declared.

"Oh, you also know about Jilqat... well, he demanded separation... He was behind the creation of a new state... well, in a way he fulfilled the aspiration of his supporters... but calling anybody a satan or devil straightaway is not right... you have to know history... you have to know and then decide; that way you can be called truly educated... Yes, I also know that those who suffered the pains of partition think Jilqat, Tarachand and others devils", Ojha stopped.

J liked the way Ojha sir was making his statement. Yes he must know more of history.

But Utpal suddenly stood up and said, "Netaji was a real hero, he was a true patriot, my father told me... He loved the country more than Tarachand or Mehra"

Ojha sir smiled, "I told you, Bengalees have a soft corner for Netaji... yes he loved his country... but whether he loved

it more than Tarachand or Mehra is very hard to ascertain...
I do not know any arithmetic, or geometry or chemistry to
figure that out"

The way Ojha sir put it made the whole class silent.

Utpal felt a bit awkward and sat down.

"Read more my children... Read more to know the
truth... History is fascinating... and the history of India,
from ancient ages to this day is really fascinating... India
witnessed the dawn of civilization, gave birth to different
cultures and religion, to science and maths, preached peace
and non-violence; yet this India witnessed tremendous
violence at different periods of history including partition..."
Ojha sir was willing to continue, but the school bell rang
indicating the end of the class.

For the first time in this school, J thought that the bell
rang too early today.

*   *   *

J and many of his classmates pursue the hobby of
collecting postage stamps. J has prepared an Album of
postage stamps. In fact Tapan-da, a book-binder in the
locality, who is also Chhorda's friend, has prepared the
Album for J. Some of his classmates like Niladri and Paul
have beautiful Albums. They have bought it from Calcutta;
from New Market, a sophisticated market place in Calcutta,
as they said. Their Albums, especially Paul's, are wonderful.
It has country-wise pages, alphabetically ordered. There are
also pages for different sizes of stamps: square, rectangular,
triangular etc. The cover of Paul's Album is dark green with
a photo of a Big Ship in Golden. It is marvelous and hugely
attractive. J likes the Album and Paul's collection very

much. But Paul never gives it to his friends. Friends can see it by sitting beside Paul in the classroom; when Paul proudly shows his collection by altering pages, and describing stamps in each page. Paul's face glows when he shows his Album to his friends. Paul has nearly 30 rectangular stamps of different countries, some known, some unknown. Paul says his maternal uncle, who stays in London, has sent these rectangular stamps for Paul. J feels jealous.

One day when J was moving his fingers over a bright rectangular stamp of flowers, desiring it to be his own, Paul promptly removed his hand and said very curtly not to do this again; it might spoil the beautiful stamp. J was hurt, very hurt, but could not say anything. Everybody in the class was afraid of Paul; he was tall, well-built and rich. J had a very ordinary collection, compared to Paul and Nilardi. J had in his possession stamps of only 15 countries, whereas they had collections from more than hundred countries. If only J had an uncle living in London, like Paul's! Even if he had a rich relative staying in Calcutta! Mejda stayed in Calcutta, but he was a poor typist struggling to earn his bread in the city. How could he buy stamps for J from the sophisticated New Market! J often dreamed that Goddess Saraswati, who looked after educational and cultural affairs among Gods, had handed over a beautiful Album, full of stamps from 200 countries to J; and Paul, Niladri and others looking enviously at the Album. But dreams never came true.

A triangular stamp fell from Paul's Album when he was showing it to friends. Paul did not notice. J took the stamp from the floor and gave it back to Paul. Paul looked at the stamp for a while, then he looked at J, and said, "Do you like it?" J nodded yes. Paul gave it to J. One corner of the triangular stamp was a bit torn, and it was also not very bright, - a soldier in an old Greek attire (like Alexander the Great, in Didi's History book) standing in a pale maroon backdrop, and the words 'Magyar Posta' was written on two sides of the stamp. What was 'Magyar Posta'? Which country's stamp was it actually? J asked Paul, but he also was not sure. He said, "I have many stamps of Magyar Posta, and I keep them under "M" in the Album. Niladri was listening to their conversation, and now he said, "Magyar Posta is a remote country in Africa, full of jungles and dreaded animals, it is a tribal land... Look at the stamp; this is the tribal king". Paul said, "How do you know?" Niladri answered, "My father told me". Niladri always referred to his father to make his statements convincing. J was very happy. This would be a prize possession in his Album. He had no triangular stamp, and also, no stamp of Magyar Posta. It would be the Sixteenth country in his Album. Paul was not as bad as J used to think of him earlier, Paul was very generous.

J flew back home that afternoon, very satisfied, immensely happy.

*   *   *

Around a month later on a rainy afternoon, Niladri, now completely cured, came to J's house. J felt very happy, as Niladri said, "no outdoor game is possible today; that's why I have come to your house to chat". J welcomed Niladri's presence. He was also getting bored with dark clouds and rains since morning. Dinka had a fever, Gundi and Utpal went outside the town, to their relatives' house. Thank God, Niladri came; otherwise this afternoon would have been boringly spoiled. Chhordi gave two pieces of hot 'roti' and 'gur' (molasses) to Niladri and J,- late afternoon tiffin. She asked Niladri whether he would like to have tea. Niladri said yes. Chhordi brought tea for them.

Fulda joined Niladri and J: "Your East Bengal won a big match last week"! He was referring to the East Bengal - Mohun Bagan Football match of the last week.

"Yes, it was possible only because Karmakar and Mazumdar played superbly", Niladri said.

J also agreed; these were two favourite footballers of J and Niladri. They were staunch supporters of East Bengal Club whose jersey was red and yellow. Mohun Bagan also had a huge support base in this town. In fact these two football teams were so associated with Bengali passion that their match always remained a big event for Bengal. People were divided into either East Bengal or Mohun Bagan. It was normally believed that people who came from East Pakistan after 1947, the 'Bangaals' supported East Bengal. Those who were originally from this part of Bengal, the 'Ghotis', used to support Mohun Bagan. Although there were exceptions, the general trend had remained so. J had never seen East Pakistan, he had never heard of East Pakistan until the refugees' arrival in their town; yet he was a supporter of East Bengal Club! Why, he was not sure. He loved its footballers, and felt happy and proud when East Bengal won. Niladri, Aziz and Gundi were also supporters of East Bengal. But Dinka, Utpal and Kabir supported Mohun Bagan.

The two small rooms in their household were full of people this afternoon. Rains prevented everybody from going out. Only Anjali ventured with the family umbrella. After some *adda* with Fulda, Niladri and J came downstairs, and sat on the big old verandah in front of other tenants' rooms. After all everything could not be discussed in front of the family elders!

Niladri said, "I have got three more stamps of Magyar Posta. Father went to Calcutta, and he purchased these for me from the New Market. I have brought these to show you. In fact I will give you one"

J became ecstatic, his stock of Magyar Posta would be two now.

Niladri said "bring your Album, I have not seen it recently. Let's see your new collections now." J rushed upstairs, and brought his Album from the big old Tin-box within minutes. Niladri took it and started to look at it very minutely.

"Oh! You don't have good new collections except a few stamps of India, and the one Paul gave to you"

"Yes", J agreed. "I don't have a good collection like you"

"I will give you a new stamp of Magyar Posta; it is very bright and colourful. Not like the pale, tattered one that Paul had given"

A wild river of happiness started flowing inside J

"Give that tattered Magyar Posta to me; in exchange I will give you another Magyar Posta. So you will have two Magyar Posta: One I will give you for free, one in exchange of the pale Magyar Posta... In fact, for me, not at all a problem... Father will go to Calcutta next month... He will bring more new stamps, including many of Magyar Posta... Now give that pale maroon one from the Album... I am giving you the new one"

J lifted the stamp Paul had given him from the Album, and gave it to Niladri.

Niladri began to see it from different angles, "Eh, this side is torn! Paul should have given you a better stamp, like me who is going to give you an absolutely fantastic one now..."

Suddenly Niladri jumped from the verandah and started to run with the maroon Magyar Posta in his hand. J was bewildered as he saw Niladri running away and gradually disappearing in the haze drizzle. J could not shout, could not cry; he only felt that irremovable lump back inside his throat. With Niladri, he saw all belief, all trust, and all faith were running away from him in the agonizing rains! For the first time in his life J felt a victim of tremendous deceit and insult. He limped back upstairs, crippled in agony and deception, with the lump stuck in his throat in that dark and rainy afternoon.

5

'SINGARA' AND CURFEW

Durga Puja is not very late this year. But there will be no 'Mahalaya Cricket'. The ground has been turned into a refugee camp. In fact refugees have taken over the ground, creating settlements for themselves. Hundreds of refugees are staying in the cricket ground and adjoining areas.

J and his friends had gone to the area a few days ago. And they were horrified. It was indeed a pathetic sight of human congregation. Makeshift ovens of mud were set up all over the place by refugees. Smoke coming out of these ovens; smell of boiling rice and vegetables along with the smell of makeshift open lavatories, created a nauseating atmosphere. Naked children playing around open lavatories, with flies perching on their unwashed faces; adult males with napkins on bare shoulders, and females with torn sari wrapped around the body; stray dogs and cows in search of food; - J had never seen such inhuman settlement of living creatures known as humans. The government provided cheap rice and potatoes to the refugees; but it had finally abandoned some failed attempts to make toilets for these people. More and more people were swamping the place everyday, and the situation went beyond control. There were reports of dysentery, malaria and enteric fever in the area. People of the town normally avoided the area for the fear of contagious diseases. Refugees have become a 'problem' not only for this town, but for the whole state of West Bengal. J read in the newspaper that the Government of India was worried over the continuing influx of refugees from East Pakistan to Assam, West Bengal, Tripura and some other border-states. J also read about hell in his story books; now he could see hell in his favourite cricket ground!

The freedom struggle in East Pakistan is continuing. An 'Independent Bangla Radio' has been created with the intention to air latest news of the freedom struggle. It also airs patriotic Bengali songs; and is a popular radio channel in West Bengal. The freedom struggle has also boosted J's urge to read the English newspaper. Now he can understand many things without Barda's help. He knows for certain now that Priti Gautam is the Prime Minister of India. He has seen her photograph in the paper; - yes she looks very beautiful. J also knows that Nirbirodh Singh is the Foreign Minister of India and Yunus Khan, a Military General is the supreme ruler of India's Western neighbour. Abdul Rahman, the leader of the Freedom Legue, is the main inspiration of the 'Mukti Fauj' (Force for Freedom) which is fighting the Pakistani army. But Barda certainly knows more, - more than even the newspaper.

J was thrilled when Barda revealed that the Indian army was helping the 'Mukti Fauj', and the Radio Station might be located somewhere in this part of the border. J felt proud when Barda said that the Indian army was very strong, and with their support, the 'Mukti Fauj' would certainly win the freedom struggle. Barda was a staunch supporter of the struggle, and so was J, and so was the rest of West Bengal, according to the Newspaper.

Durga Puja is much mellowed this year. Every Puja Committee has cut down the budget to help the refugees. Voluntary organizations are collecting clothes and food for the refugees. J and his friends are also part of the collection group of their local club. All families in the locality have contributed whatever they could. J has no regret for Mahalaya cricket; if 'Mukti Fauj' wins, they would organize big cricket next year. Some elders of the locality are saying that both parts of Bengal, East and West will be reunited again, and the Bengalees would emerge as a strong nationality. Some are even fancying that they may get back their lost property in the Eastern part, which they had left in 1947.

Mother came back from her usual stroll one evening, and asked Barda, "Heard that everybody would get back their lost property after the war... true?" Chances of getting back property aroused mother's interest in the freedom struggle.

Barda said, "almost impossible... these are only rumours... spread by people who are detached from reality"

"Oh! Hell with the struggle then", mother went for a wash.

"Barda, is it true that both parts of Bengal would be united again?" J asked

"A fancy again", Barda replied, "look you should know that India was divided on the basis of religion; and that religious sentiment would exist". Barda was remarkable, J thought, not only for his wisdom, but also for his tenacity to explain everything to J, whom others considered (including mother) too little to know everything!

Situation worsened in East Pakistan after the Pujas. With struggle intensifying, refugees entering into India almost doubled. Priti Gautam requested Pakistan to settle the issue, and to stop the influx of refugees to India. Her government felt that Indian economy and society were hit hard by this influx. Priti appealed to world leaders to intervene and solve the crisis. The Americans were behind Pakistan, J came to know from the newspaper, because Pakistan was an American ally in this part of the world. J now became very curious about the struggle, and also news surrounding the struggle, like the stances America and Russia had taken on the issue of the freedom struggle in East Pakistan. One evening Fulda and Barda were having a conversation over the issue and J was listening silently with rapt attention

"You see, the Americans are supporting Pakistan, the oppressors", Fulda told Barda

"Yes the Americans always support Pakistan", Barda replied

"Don't worry, the Russians are behind India"

"You should not say Russia", Barda said, "you are now in college; it is not Russia, it is the Soviet Union. That is the proper name"

"Well, well. It is all the same", Fulda continued, "The Soviet Union will support India"

"Yes, they have signed a treaty with India... the Friendship Treaty... It says they will support India in case of any attack".

J became curious... Could India be attacked? He thought, but remained silent.

"Yes I have also read in the newspaper about the treaty", Fulda said, "it is very good for India".

"At least it will scare away Pakistan and deter America", Barda said with all seriousness

"Down with America, they are the spoilers everywhere in the world. And that man, their leader... looks like a shopkeeper ... he does not like India or Priti Gautam", Fulda looked very excited.

J knew exactly the name of the leader of the United States of America and he silently appreciated his own knowledge.

"Yes, he has the interest of his own shop, America in mind". Barda paused a little, and continued, "But I can tell you that America is not a spoiler. It also fought colonial powers, and struggled to build a nation. Now it is ahead in science and technology, in arts and culture, in music and films... well, only one man does not make the whole of America".

"But Brezinski is superb. Look how he is behind India", Fulda would not give up.

"Yes, he is a very strong leader".

A few days ago, J saw the picture of Brezinski, a large-faced individual. His photo surely revealed that he was powerful and strong. J silently supported Barda's statement.

"I don't understand why America is always against India", Fulda exclaimed.

"This is politics, you know", Barda continued, "firstly, Pakistan is their friend; and secondly they don't like India's policy of non-alignment".

J became very inquisitive, "what is non-alignment, Barda", he broke his silence.

"Oh! the smart chap again", Fulda said rudely.

"Let him know, this way he can develop his ideas", Barda said, and continued, "America and Soviet Union are the two strong countries in the world, and each of them expects all other nations of the world to support them. But India supports neither... India is not committed to anyone".

But India supports Russia... err... Soviet Union...you were talking about the treaty..." J asked instantly.

"Well... well... it is true that India is now close to Soviet Union; but officially it has not joined any bloc; - Soviet or American".

"He is right Barda" Fulda said, "how can India be non-committal if it signs a treaty with Soviet Union?"

"Well, you see it is a Friendship Treaty... there is no harm in going for friendship", Barda sounded like the Indian Foreign Minister.

"But it talks of help in case of any attack, it is almost a defence treaty", the college student in Fulda protested.

"Well, you are partly right... well, India is compelled by the situation now... the situation in East Pakistan and the American support to the Pakistani Administration".

J was relishing the discussion, but Chhordi called him for dinner. As per norms of the household, the younger ones, J, Pari and Bhai used to take dinner in the first batch; others in the next one.

Winter has set in early this year. Chilly winds and dry skin, arrival of oranges, notice for annual examination, ruthless brown trees lurking in the blue sky - all signaling an early winter.

*   *   *

"We had to prepone the annual exam... the situation is not good... with so many refugees in town, the school building could be taken over by the government to shelter the refugees…" A grim Headmaster announced

"If it had been taken over already", Banku whispered in J's ear.

"The Bengali-speaking people in East Pakistan are fighting for a separate country, as you know", Ghosal sir, the Headmaster of the school continued, "and refugees are coming, they are all over, as you can see… The District Magistrate has met us and told us that the school may be taken over to give shelter to the refugees… the situation is not good at all… I know preparing for the exam in this disturbing condition is very difficult…"

"Then why don't you cancel the exam", Banku whispered again.

"…but this school has a reputation… a tradition… it is the best in the district… we will try to maintain our standard… Prepare yourself boys, prepare for the exam as well as for the tough time ahead. God bless you", Ghosal sir ended his small speech. The boys came back to their classroom. Ojha sir would meet them to discuss few points from his course. J loved Ojha sir's class.

"You heard what the Headmaster said", the dhoti-clad Ojha told the boys, "the situation is in fact alarming. There are prospects of a war…"

"War? Between whom?" many boys asked in chorus.

"Between India and Pakistan", Ojha sir continued, "India told Pakistan to control the situation in the Eastern part and stop the influx of refugees. India got affected for trouble in Pakistan. Indian economy was hit hard. But Pakistan had alleged that India was interfering into its internal matter. India said that it was no longer an internal issue of Pakistan because India got affected in a big way.

India also urged the world community to help diffuse tension in East Pakistan"

"Yes, Nirbirodh Singh is travelling to different parts of the world", J proudly said.

"You read the newspaper daily, which paper?" Ojha asked.

"The Morning Nectar", J said loudly.

"That's good. All of you should read the newspaper regularly… yes J is right… Nirbirodh Singh, our Foreign Minister is travelling to different countries to tell their leaders about India's woeful plight due to the trouble in East Pakistan… But Pakistan is accusing India of instigating trouble in the Eastern part of Pakistan", Ojha paused

"When will the war take place Sir", Kamal asked, "I like wars… I have seen a film on war… planes fly and throw missiles… I like to see planes fly that way… Pilots are so brave…" Kamal gestured to show, stretching his two hands and bending his body, how planes fly.

"No, wars are not good, they kill many people", Gagan protested.

"Gagan is right", Ojha said, "people are killed, many lose their dear ones, thousands of people are displaced from their homelands… wars are horrible".

"Then why do countries fight wars?" Aziz asked.

"That is the most puzzling question to answer", Ojha continued, "everyone knows that wars are bad, yet wars take place frequently… when interests of the nations clash, wars take place".

"Interest of the nation, what is that", J asked.

"As you boys fight when you can't agree on a certain issue, nations also fight when they disagree… when they have conflicting interests", Ojha replied. "But the annual exam is important... we hope we can follow the new schedule", Ojha diverted the issue much to the dislike of J and his classmates.

"Sir tell us more about war", Kamal pleaded.

"I will tell you more about the syllabus now... syllabus for the exam...write it down... chapters 1 to 8, the full book".

"It would be too heavy Sir", Banku said.

"Don't worry", Arunava quipped "war is nearer, and you will not have to study at all, forget the whole book. War has positive sides also".

Everybody including Ojha sir laughed at Arunava's comments.

But the situation in East Pakistan has worsened further. The Mukti Fauj wants a separate state, 'Bangladesh' for the Bengali-speaking population. The military government in Pakistan is against the demand, and trying to suppress it. The Mukti Fauj has full support of India, which is backed by Soviet Union. Priti Gautam has issued a warning to Pakistan that India would not merely watch the situation because India got affected directly by the problems in East Pakistan. J almost devours these news items now-a-days. He even reports some 'special' items to Barda after he comes back home.

J had reported last evening that the Mukti Fauj got hold of a town near Dhaka and waived its flag there. J heard this news from the radio in the afternoon. He felt elated to be the first one to break the news to Barda when he returned home in the evening. Barda brought some "Singara" (snacks) and he gave J two hot singaras, for his interest in current affairs. J was delighted. Oh, hot singara in the winter evening! They tasted most delicious in the winter because freshly cooked cauliflowers, peas, onion and potatoes were stuffed inside the triangle outer layer of flours. Cauliflowers and peas were only available in winter! J liked the taste of early winter cauliflowers.

Suddenly Pari started crying because there was a shortage of singaras as Barda gave one 'extra' to J. Pari had to share one singara with Bhai who also vociferously supported Pari's plea. Pari was accusing Barda of pampering J at the cost of other sisters and brothers. Barda also started shouting, and said, "what if the youngest in the family gets an extra?... I have done nothing wrong"

"Eh, nothing wrong", taunted Pari, "One is getting more... and the others are starving", Pari's howling became louder.

"You are starving? You all are having singaras... That's why I don't bring anything", Barda shouted.

"I know, you bring sweets everyday on your way back from office, and secretly give those to that devil", Pari pointed towards J.

"Is that true?" Anjali joined the circus, "unimaginable, dastardly act..."

"Yes, I have seen many times... but did not tell you... Today I am so upset... that I can't help telling you", Pari got more strength to yell more loudly.

"Oh, I bring sweets from our office tiffin club... not daily... but occasionally... I do not eat my quota... and bring those for J...", Barda said.

"Eh, the liar... he purchases sweets for the devil... now can't tell the truth when caught", Pari got a chance to humiliate Barda.

"Shame, shame... that is why that little devil has become so dangerous", Anjali quipped.

"I am not supposed to answer you everything", Barda said forcefully, "I am the eldest... I am the earner... I am not answerable to you... however you can have my singara if you like".

"Why should I have your quota. This is a question of justice...this a question of equal distribution", Pari was sound in her argument.

"And that is a question of love, that is a question of affection for the youngest in the family", Barda was unrepentant, "I said you can have my singara".

"Eh, already had one, where is his quota... showing generosity..." Anjali grinned.

"Already had one? Me?" Barda wondered.

"I saw you eating one while entering the house", Anjali sounded like a clever detective this time.

"You liar, you saw me eating one... I will kill you", Barda shouted

"Kill me, you can only do that... kill all sisters... and pamper all brothers... that is your only motto", Now Anjali also started crying.

Mother appeared from almost nowhere; she came back after her evening stroll and entered silently, almost unnoticed. For a few seconds, she observed everything, and then started shouting: "illiterate, greedy goats, creating a hell for singaras" she looked towards Pari and Anjali.

"Eh, the Pundit has arrived", Chhordi quipped, "how can the children of an illiterate mother be scholars?"

"You 'petni', you ugly ghost, you stop... look, my sons are brilliant" Mother shouted back.

Now Chhordi started crying, "Oh God! what a mother! calling her own child ugly... not only ugly, but also a ghost"

"Yes, ugly and ghost, together", mother clarified.

Chhordi started cursing her birth and her luck.

"Where is my singara?" Mother asked Barda.

"Nothing left, all gone", Bhai quipped.

"Look, I only called these petnis greedy for nothing", mother pointed towards her daughters; "ate everything, left nothing for the only mother".

"Only mother!" Fulda joined the show, "how many mothers can we expect to have?"

"Oh God! not only greedy, but obscene… I know you have become very indecent, very obscene after you got into that college".

"I learned obscenity from you", Fulda got angry for castigating his college.

"Oh God, where are you? Look for whom I steal, calls me a thief", mother went back to her favourite proverb.

"You don't have to steal for us", Fulda retorted.

"Tit for tat… getting her due from the beloved sons", Anjali retorted.

"Why are you interfering, illiterate goat?", Mother shouted back, "it is between me and my son".

"Mad, complete mad; totally insane! Otherwise one can't be so rude to her daughters", Pari said in a philosopher's voice.

"You call me mad?" Mother rushed towards Pari and a little scuffle followed.

Clash of interest… leads to war… Ojha's words came to J's mind all of a sudden. But what is the interest here? Singara? The urge to dominate? Madness may also lead to war, thought J. He wished he could blurt out all singaras, and give them back to his 'deprived' siblings. Singara turned out to be hugely acidic in this winter evening.

* * *

'Curfew' has been declared in the town. A new word to J; - he quickly writes it down in his hand-made 'khata' (exercise book) which he has titled 'vocabulary'. Whenever he reads about or listens to a new English word, he writes it down in his 'vocabulary' khata. Curfew is a situation where normal activities are disrupted; people cannot go out of home, they cannot assemble on road, J has learnt from Barda. Special announcements have been made by the municipality urging people to shut their windows so that lights may not be seen from outside. Now after evening, lights on the roads are not switched on. Headlights of all motor vehicles are painted black on the upper. They look quite funny at daytime. The circular headlight is divided into two parts, one black, the upper part, and the lower portion is normal glass of the headlight. This has been specially done so that enemy planes cannot see any light from the sky.

This small town is not very lighted in any case; motor vehicles are few, mostly government vehicles, and they do not normally ply at night. Yet all motor vehicles have been ordered to paint their headlights black on the upper part. The war has finally started, in this December, when windows are normally shut for cold weather. This is a natural advantage. If enemy planes see light from the sky, they will bomb the area. So the whole town gets immersed in darkness after evening. Dinka has informed his friends last morning that elders in his house do not talk loudly anymore; they only whisper. They only whisper about rising prices, and scarcity of essentials if war continues. An atmosphere of fear is everywhere. But where are the diving planes? Where are the dust-bursting bombs? Only curfew, only restriction to go out! Is this war? It is not at all exciting. Barda says that big cities like Delhi, Calcutta, Bombay are more vulnerable. They would be bombed first by the enemy; then small towns. Small towns might even be spared. J thanks his luck and God; he lives in a small town!

Radio is the main source of news in every household. Thankfully Barda has purchased a new 'Philips' radio before 'Mahalaya' this year. The old 'Murphy' radio has got a higher pedestal, literally; it has been placed permanently on the top of the old wooden Almirah, an honourable retirement. Newspapers normally reach this small town in late afternoon, between 2 to 3 p.m. They come by the morning train from Calcutta. The train is run by steam engine. The train is slow, and made more slower due to the 'single' line that connects this small town with Calcutta. The train has to stop in many stations for 'crossing' trains coming from opposite direction. It takes 7 to 8 hours to reach this town from Calcutta. Even that train is uncertain now due to war. Newspapers may or may not come. Therefore Radio has become the primary source of news, -news about war. Everybody in every household sits around the radio, and listens to news about the war. In between patriotic songs which are now frequently aired, the news reader narrates how the Indian army is fighting a glorious war; and how the Indian air force is 'covering' them.

But in J's house, there is another palpable tension. All in the family are apprehensive about Chhorda being sent to the war by military authorities.

"I can't think anymore, I can't bear this life anymore", Ma was telling Barda last night. "I suffered partition, faced starvation, humiliation, struggled to see my children grow up… and now my son would go to war… and get killed… That I can't bear anymore… That's why I have become mad". Tears rolled down mother's eyes. J was also in tears; but he wiped his tears secretly.

"Don't worry", Barda consoled mother, "he is not in the combat division, he may not be dispatched".

"I don't believe… luck has betrayed me always… I am waiting for the worst… Did you get any news of him?"

"Not yet… I am waiting for his post card", Barda said, "That's the reason why I always listen to the radio".

"What is the radio saying about the war?" Ma asked.

"Indian army is doing well", Barda replied.

"Has it announced the names of the soldiers sent to the war front?", Ma enquired.

"It is not possible to announce every name", Barda said.

"Does it declare the names of dead soldiers?", Ma seemed desperate.

"Sometimes it does".

"Have you heard the names recently?"

"Oh Ma, be cool, be normal".

"Is the postal service normal now"? Mother asked with worries writ large all over her face.

"Army has a special service; they send their mails in a special way", Barda said.

"Has any mail come today?"

"No Ma, probably it will come tomorrow".

"It will never come, I know… It will never come… my son is already in the war… you are hiding things from me… is he still alive? Tell me the truth… Is he still alive?" mother looked hysteric now. Barda quickly caught hold of her, and she fainted. Chhordi rushed with a bucket of water and a 'pankha' (hand fan). She knew how to tackle such situations.

J quickly slid to bed, unnoticed. He could not watch things anymore. Wars were really bad...Wars killed people, I knew ; but I never imagined that a war could kill my own brother...Wars were horrible, extremely painful...J dipped his face in the pillow...He did not want anybody to see that he was crying...that he was bleeding inside, that the smart boy was losing a war with himself this evening.

6

THIRD WORLD WAR

One week had passed, and the war seemed to be going in India's favour, at least if the radio was to be believed. The Indian army was advancing well into East Pakistan and capturing many areas. Curfew was on, and therefore lights were off at night on the roads of this small town. Only one helicopter flew over this town in the last week, that too during daytime. The loud noise of the helicopter brought some curious young boys to the roof-tops, and roads; but they were quickly reprimanded by the elders. They had to go inside fearing bombing from the sky, and from the elders. There was no vertical bombing from above, although at the ground level, there were many from family elders. And the lone helicopter 'exploded' several bombs of rumour. According to Dinka's father, the helicopter was carrying Priti Gautam for an inspection of the war zone, through this border district. Utpal's father: injured army men were being taken to the hospital; Gundi's uncle: It was going to drop bombs in East Pakistan; Kabir's Grandfather: Russian army was inspecting the area, because they would join the war in support of the Indian army; Barun's mother: It was a spy helicopter from Pakistan, very ominous for this town, because this town would be bombed soon. J's friends carried all the messages from respective households. After a lot of debate in the clubroom (locked from inside), Barun's mother emerged the winner. The helicopter actually was a spy one from Pakistan; it surveyed their town, and was ready to bomb the town anytime. The gathering quickly dispersed. Curfew was there; but more importantly, it was better to be in the family during bombing so that everybody could die united.

Another major fear, no less detrimental than bombing, was the risk of the rising prices of essential commodities. Sankarda came to J's house yesterday and told Barda that supply trucks were few to the town due to war and there could be a scarcity of goods. He advised Barda to stock essentials. Barda said that if every household tried to stock things, goods would vanish very soon. Sankarda alleged that everybody was trying to store essentials. Sankarda knew the reality because his two nephews had small business shops in the market. Later that day, government officials made mobile announcements from cycle-rickshaws that nobody should panic and store essentials; there was no shortage of goods in this town. They requested people not to panic on the basis of rumours, and warned the traders not to create artificial scarcity by storing essentials.

"The situation is not good", Barda said grimly that evening, "we have to consume less rice, less daal (pulses), infact everything... very judiciously". All agreed, but Bhai whispered into J's ear: "we will have one roti at night instead of three".

"The situation would be out of control", Barda said, "if the war continues".

But one thing Barda could bring under control very effectively, in fact, very effectively. It was mother's anxieties for Chhorda. Barda told Ma that the Post Card from Chhorda had finally arrived; he was not sent to the war. Ma wanted to see the Post Card, and Barda showed Ma a not-too-old Post Card written by Chhorda in pre-war days. Barda even read from that Post Card, every single ward J could remember distinctly:

> **"Dear Ma,**
>
> **I am well. Don't worry, I have not been sent to the war front. Yesterday my officer said that our division would not be sent to the war, as we are a non-combat division... my friends Thapa, Singh, Rawat, and Aslam... I told you about them several times... brave guys... all from the combat division... have already gone to the war... if they had me and our division in mind, we would have been dispatched already as well... Thank God, I'm in the non-combat division... But I am concerned about my friends... How are you? Hope others in the family are well... My regards to you and Barda, love to the juniors... your son..."**

How Barda read it without any hesitation? Did he rehearse early? Everybody listened in revered silence. Ma appeared contended and relieved. J thanked God because mother was illiterate! Later that evening Chhordi told J:

"Our Barda is like 'Yudhistir' in the 'Mahabharata', the Epic mythology. Like 'Yudhistir', he is also the eldest, and like 'Yudhistir' again, he had to tell an important lie to manage the situation and restore order". One Post Card and one lie made Barda bigger than 'Yudhistir' in the family.

America has sent a naval war-ship to help Pakistan in the war, and the ship is heading towards the Bay of Bengal. India and many other countries in the world are angry over this American strategy. A Soviet combat fleet is reported to be following the American ship. J and his friends, in fact the whole town, are debating the possibility of a Third World War with huge concern and interest. The Second World War ended in 1945, J knows; that means twenty five years have passed without a World War. Wars are very bad, J and his friends now agree. But Kabir has told the other day that if the Third World War started in the Bay of Bengal, this part of the world would find a place in history. That proposition sounded lucrative to many.

"OK, we will die, but the whole area would remain alive in history", Barun began the discussion in one foggy morning.

"Can an area remain alive, if all human beings are dead?" J asked.

"Other animals would be there, the monkeys, cows, dogs, cats", Dinka said.

"No, No all animals would die in bombing, a World War is huge, very dangerous, unlike small wars", Gundi gave his verdict.

"You are wrong, some animals will definitely survive", Dinka said, "those who live under the ground, - snakes, ants, rats, earthworms etc".

"You fool, Russia has prepared bombs that can go deep down the earth, and destroy everything; in fact water comes out from below the earth if that bomb is dropped", Barun said very seriously.

"He is right, if Third World War breaks out, there will be no earth... I mean no land... all would be turned into water... I read in a book", Utpal now joined the discussion.

"Then animals who live in water would survive... many reptiles live in water... they will survive", Dinka is determined to support the reptiles.

"That is a possibility", Barun said.

"If human beings could live in water"! Kabir lamented.

"Actually humans are the most helpless lot among the animals on earth... they will die early in the case of a Third World War", Aziz, the judge gave his verdict.

"No, No, they are the most intelligent", Gundi protested.

"What intelligence would do if bombs destroy everything and the earth is filled with water"? Utpal asked, "Can we remain in water for long? We can't... so we will die in any case... die of bombing in the land... and in water... oh! I can't think more".

The group came to a conclusion that poor human beings were the most helpless creatures on earth at times of catastrophe. Dinka said that during war, it was better to be an ant than a human being. J silently supported Dinka.

More than ten days had passed since the war started; and it seemed India was heading towards a victory. Indian soldiers, along with the Mukti Fauj, had captured many areas from the Pakistani military. The Fauj had established its control over those areas. America, contrary to expectations by a large section of people in the subcontinent, had not joined the war in favour of Pakistan. The American ship remained stationed in the Bay of Bengal, and the U.S. said that the ship was sent to evacuate all Americans trapped in East Pakistan. Very few in India and East Pakistan accepted the American argument.

The Freedom Legue had already declared that East Pakistan would be named "Bangladesh", an independent country of the Bengalee-speaking people, and Dhaka would be its capital. Victory was near, the Freedom Legue also declared, as reports of more and more Pakistani army surrendering and retreating emerged. J and his friends were also jubilant at the prospect of an Indian victory, although at the inner corner of everbody's mind, pain for a missed Third World War remained. At the beginning of the war, nobody thought that Pakistan would lose the war so early.

"Priti Gautam has done a miracle", Sankarda, who visited J's house almost regularly, told Barda in one pleasant morning. Golden rays of the Sun were peeping through the 'Neem' tree in this chilly December morning, as Chhordi offered a cup of tea to Sankar. "Yes Mr. Swamy told me in the market that Priti G surpassed Banwari Lal Mehra as a leader", Barda replied.

"Definitely, during Mehra's tenure India lost the war against China, and staggered in another war some years later. But look, Priti Gautam brought a respectful victory for India in this war", Sankar was beaming with Priti G's success. The radio reported last night that the Pakistani Commander-in-Chief would formally surrender today to the Indian Commander-in-Chief, and the whole of India was ecstatic. Curfew had been relaxed in day-time, and people everywhere were discussing about Priti Gautam.

"The lady is not only beautiful, she is very determind", Sankar continued, "ah! this tea is also beautiful".

"But I am not", Chhordi replied.

"One who serves good hot tea in a chilly morning is always beautiful", Sankar replied.

"Don't tell lies, blatant lies... instead tell more about Priti... She is a real angel", Chhordi said, "a lady at the top... it is really a matter of pride for all women in India", Chhordi told from heart.

"She is Goddess Durga, incarnated", Mother joined the fray.

"Yes, Aunty is absolutely right. Priti G can only be compared to Goddess Durga. As Durga demolished "Mahishasur", the Demon, Priti demolished the Pakistanis, bigger demons", Sankar said forcefully.

"But think of those Pakistani soldiers who died in the war", Barda told gently.

"Oh Barda, everyone would think that you are a Pakistani, if you say like this. In a war soldiers would die; that is natural... and Pakistan has always been our enemy. Are you not happy at the Indian victory?" Sankar questioned.

"Yes, I am also happy. But last night I was thinking that if we were so concerned about our brother going to war, so were several Pakistani families... many of their sons and brothers had gone to war and got killed. I feel pained when I think of them", Barda replied.

"Don't tell this to anybody what you have told me", Sankar advised, "You would be branded as a Pakistani agent".

"I know, but wars are really horrible... I have grown a deep hatred for war, at this time of victory" Barda said grimly. J looked at Barda, and the 'over-smart' in J realized that all pains inside Barda had assembled on his face.

"Can I have another cup of tea"? Sankar said, "the tea is beautiful... besides, we have to celebrate India's glorious victory".

"I will have to prepare", Chhordi said.

"Prepare another round of tea for all of us. Hey J won't you like a cup of tea again?" Sankar asked. "He already had his quota... children should not drink excessive tea", Chhordi said, "I will give you and Barda another round".

"Okay, but make the tea more beautiful this time", Sankar looked very vibrant this morning.

"I can't guarantee, but I will try", Chhordi replied.

"After testing this round, I will invite Priti G to have a cup of tea in this household", Sankar joked and started laughing at his own comments, as Chhordi slid into the kitchen.

India had recognized Bangladesh as an independent nation. Bhutan and Soviet Union also recognized Bangladesh. Newspaper supply had become regular, as well as life, in this small town. J was happily immersed again in gathering more news about the post-war situation, and the newly independent country. The newspapers were full of praise for Priti Gautam. It was a remarkable victory for India, and it was possible due to the effective and able leadership of Priti. From a weak military in the early 1960s, and largely ineffective power during the middle of the decade, Priti turned her nation into a strong regional power, the newspaper commented. A feel-good factor had embraced the nation, and every household in this small town. Before the Christmas holidays, annual exam results came out. J stood first in his section. This year nobody failed, all his classmates were promoted to Grade VI, more good news indeed! Chhorda's 'real' letter had finally arrived, he was not sent to the war front. Barda showed the 'real' letter to Ma on the Christmas day: "Ma, I lied to you earlier, to keep you free of tension. That was not the real letter from D. Here is the 'real' one; it came yesterday. Sorry Ma".

"I knew that was not the real letter", Ma stunned Barda, and J, who followed Barda to Ma.

"Did anybody tell you?" Barda asked.

"Nobody... but I realized that you were faking to keep me happy... And I also pretended... I tried to gather mental strength... I told God before that if I broke down for one son, what would happen to my other children... I had witnessed several deaths... suffered many pains in '47... I prayed to God to give me strength to witness more... you did the best thing under the circumstances... but I realized... You know, illiterates have sixth sense... they can also understand what the literates are up to... but you have done nothing wrong..." Ma stopped.

"Sorry Ma", Barda said.

"Read today's letter... I hope this is not the false one", Ma laughed.

"No Ma, not at all", Barda said.

"Give the Post card to J, he will read it, I know he loves these jobs", Ma told Barda.

J was indeed very happy to read the letter for Ma. After he finished, Ma patted him on the shoulders and asked him to take two 'Narus' (sweets) made of coconut. J was very very happy. Mother was different; she was not that insane as J had thought earlier; she did have a heart, and also a brain, -she loved her children too. Nothing could be better at this year-end except the news that Bhai failed again in class VIII, third time in a row, and he might be expelled from the school. Barda enquired in other schools; they were also reluctant to admit a thrice-failed student in an upper class. Except for this news the year-end would have been fantastic for J. India's victory in the war, J's success in the annual exam, promotion of all his friends to the next class, coconut sweets, and above everything, - the grand discovery of his own mother made J very happy. Without any war and with love and affection flowing abundantly, life was indeed beautiful!

7

CHICKEN POX AND LIZARDS

Three matches of inter-district cricket tournament would be played in J's town this year. These matches were scheduled to be played in December but due to the war and refugee problem, it would finally start in early March. Three 'home' matches for their district was also a bonus for J and his friends after the grand year end. Matches would be played at the big ground in the middle of the town. Refugees were not allowed to settle at this ground because all big government officials, - the Distirct Magistrate, the Superintendent of Police, the District Judge, the Sub Divisional Officer, -and many other high officials of the district lived in bungalows around this big ground. A part of this ground was getting covered now with long pieces of tin placed in between bamboo sticks. This town, unlike many other towns, had no permanent stadium. For every 'big' game, cricket or football, such arrangements were always made. J and his friends noticed yesterday on their way back from school that almost half of the playing area had been covered with tin. The first match would start on March 7; the second and third games were scheduled for March 10 and 12. The whole school, including its teachers, was excited this year because Hapa, who was adjudged the Best School cricketer, had been selected in the district team. Ghosh sir, the sports teacher of the school, was elated at Hapa's selection. Sir often told junior boys that Hapa would be a big cricketer in future. Sir saw in Hapa another Anil Salaskar, - the famous batsman of the Indian cricket team, - in the making.

But Hapa was not short like Salaskar, he was tall, bright and handsome. J saw him bat in many inter-school games. He came to bat at the No. 4 position. The way he entered the ground was terrific. He did not wear a helmet; and the collar of his white cricketing shirt was always up; the upper most button of the shirt kept open, a white cloth was wrapped round his neck as he walked to the pitch tossing the bat from one hand to another. Ghosh sir said that at 17, Hapa had a well built and stout figure. Hapa was already a hero in the school but he seldom attended the school; he was busy in cricketing activities. The Headmaster had allowed him to play; - he was after all the pride of the school. But whenever he came to school, juniors had jostled to see him, to talk to him. But Hapa did not talk to anybody except teachers. He used to go straight to Ghosh sir's room; Often Ghosh sir took him to Headmaster's room, and after some time, he was off in his motorbike. He was very good looking, like Sobhan Pilot, the wicket keeper of the Indian team. But he was compared to Salaskar by everybody, probably due to his batting skills.

J was little upset because tin-cover in the ground meant that there would be an entry-fee for the matches. This time all students not allowed for free; only players representing schools in different games (football, cricket, volleyball, badminton) would be allowed free. But a reduction in fee for students was announced, - fifty paisa per game. J calculated that he had only seventy paisa in his earthen pot where he normally saved coins. That meant he could manage only one game; for the other two, he needed eighty paisa more. In his group Niladri and Utpal would be able to see all the games. Gundi's father worked in the DM.'s office and got one free pass. So Gundi could also watch all the games, but others were unsure, like J. However, Utpal was sure that Hapa would definitely score a century in any of the matches, if not in all. J had prayed to God so that Hapa got a century in the first match that J was going to witness.

Three days before the first match, J and his friends made a round of the make-shift 'stadium' to see if there was any gap in between tins. Aziz and Barun were especially interested; they could not collect any money; they planned to peep through the gaps. But they found no gap this year. Ah God, why there were no gaps? How could they see matches! They made a last-ditch effort to find gaps in between erected sheets of tin. Four volunteers rushed to them when they were about to finish their 'inspection' of the make-shift 'stadium', and told them not to go near the tin-barricades. Aziz gestured at them, and they chased J's gang. Other volunteers also joined. J and his friends ran fast to get out of their reach. And then it started raining all of a sudden, and they got thoroughly drenched. Aziz and Barun shouted at the volunteers to say that rains would spoil the game. God would bring rains to spoil the volunteers' bid to prevent poor boys from watching the game.

"But in that case Hapa will not get his century", Dinka suddenly said, with rain drops all over his face.

"Who cares, said Aziz, "when I am not inside, it matters little to me whether Hapa gets his century or not".

"I will try to manage a pass for you", Gundi said.

"But what will happen to Barun"? Aziz asked, "you certainly cannot manage two more passes".

"Let's see", Gundi replied in a low, uncertain voice.

"We can climb up the adjacent tree", Barun suggested, "year before last, I saw a game from the tree-top".

"This year there would be heavy police guard… no one would be allowed to climb up the tree", Dinka said with all wisdom.

"I will see the game at any cost… that is my challenge", Barun said throwing his arms in the rains. J's friends loved to take 'challenge', and they took huge pride in proclaiming and announcing these 'challenges'. The rains intensified and appeared to be challenging as well for the game and the town.

J came home that evening fully drenched. Chhordi began to shout at him, but simultaneously started to wipe him with a napkin. J went to the bathroom for a change, but felt a shiver within. He came out quickly and enquired whether there was any tea. Chhordi gave him a cup of hot tea. J now felt better. Chhordi gave him two rotis. J rolled and dipped the rotis inside the tea, and quickly ate them one after the other. He was getting late for his studies. It might generate another round of scolding J knew, because Bhai and Pari had already started their studies. But after about fifteen minutes since he sat for studies, J felt very sleepy and began to droop. Within minutes, he fell on Bhai's lap. Bhai was trying to make him sit again, but could not. He now shouted "J has fever, his body is damn hot".

"I knew", Chhordi shouted back… "got drenched at this awesome time of the year, when the season is changing".

"Taking him to bed", Fulda said, and immediately lifted J to bed.

The fever continued, and by the next day rashes came out all over J's body.

"Chicken Pox", Ma pronounced, "fix the mosquito net over the cot near the window".

"But one single, segregated bed for him is difficult to afford", Anjali quipped.

"I will sleep with him", Ma said. "You can sleep in the room if you like, or you can sleep in the other room or the verandah" Ma suggested.

"But it is still cold... sleeping in the verandah...", Anjali said.

"I will sleep in the verandah", Bhai offered.

"I will sleep there too", Fulda said.

"We have to manage you see... we have to be cautious also... chicken pox is contagious... it is common at this time of the year... but we should not be afraid... we have to fight any disease and survive", Ma sounded unusually calm.

For the next seven days J was almost unconscious with high fever and pain. He did not know how he had taken food, or gone to the toilet. He could only remember that he had a dream one night: Hapa scored a century in the first match and Barun, dancing in joy, fell from the tree, but remained (thank God) unhurt. Nothing else he could remember. Now after a week, he came back to his senses. The fever and pain subsided, but the rashes remained, and started itching. It was very boring to stay inside the mosquito net always, with few people around, especially during day time. Others were busy outside; and Chhordi and Ma heavily engaged in the kitchen. J was desperate to know the results of the match; but nobody in the household was interested. If only he could contact his friends! But they would not come to J before he was completely cured, chicken pox was very infectious.

After another week, J was permitted to read storybooks. He was given his favourite detective series, written by one Pawan Kumar. He was very popular among the High School boys. His main characters, Rupak Chatterjee the Detective, and Maganlal, the Detective's Assistant, solved all mysteries and crimes at the end of the story. Pawan Kumar published a series of books, - thin, with colourful attractive pictures in the cover, and thrilling stories inside. These were hot favourites among boys. But J was allowed to read only one book a day. Otherwise his eyes and body would be under strain, Barda opined. But J finished reading the thin book within an hour. J normally read the book after lunch, because when the story finally ended, J used to feel very drowsy, and quickly fell asleep.

J finished ten detective stories in the last ten days. Even Pawan Kumar had become boring now. J himself solved the crime yesterday before he finished "Kalo Barir Rahasya" (Mystery inside the Black House). He guessed rightly that the beautiful lady, who looked innocent, was the murderer. At the end, J proved right, and he became very excited and proud. He was no less intelligent than Pawan Kumar, and he decided to write detective stories, - more efficiently than Pawan Kumar, - once he got cured. He would earn huge fame by his stories, like Agatha Christie or Arthur Conan Doyle, the two most famous detective story writers J knew. Nobody would be able to guess anything from his stories until the last paragraph! Oh, when he would be cured, and start his stories! He had even planned the title of his first book: "Night in the Graveyard"! Oh, the very title was so thrilling and awe-evoking! He wanted some papers and a pen inside his mosquito net. But he was heavily scolded. Elders were so cruel and frustrating at times!

A lot of things were happening in the world outside, but J was confined within the mosquito net. Nothing could be more boring. J asked Fulda about the results of the cricket matches, but Fulda said, "Don't know, not interested". Fulda was a geek; he knew nothing beyond his studies. J asked Bhai, and Bhai said, "Don't tell me about cricket, I hate that game; I love football". In desperation, J asked Barda, and Barda said "probably our district lost... but I'm not sure... I will tell you later". Our district lost! That meant Hapa could not score a century! What about Ashraf's lethal spin bowling? Barda was not sure... he did not know... our team could not lose. By the time J would be fit to go out, all the matches would be finished... Oh, God, such a bad luck for J!

On the twenty first day since pox was detected, J was permitted to take a bath. Chhordi and Ma took him to the bathroom in order to apply turmeric paste all over his body. J felt very awkward and shy to stand naked in front of Ma and Chhordi. But Ma was really shameless. She pulled down J's shorts quickly. J tried to pull it up, and Chhordi began to laugh:

"Look our little brother is feeling shy", she told Ma.

"It happens at this age; but ignore him, and apply turmeric paste all over his body".

J stood naked and helpless in front of the cruel, elderly ladies. But soon he realized that the smell of turmeric was not so bad and began to like it. But he hated the way Chhordi and Ma were applying it all over his body. Moreover, he did not like the yellowish shade of the skin caused by turmeric. But turmeric was good after chicken pox, elders always said.

Tomorrow he would be permitted to go out. It would be a Sunday tomorrow; so all his friends would be there in the club-room in the morning. Ah, finally fresh air! Last three weeks J was almost like a prisoner, confined to a small cell. Now he could also start his detective novel. He would start his novel from next evening. He had already planned the crime plot. It was a terrific plot; everybody would be startled and shocked after reading the novel. Nobody would be able to guess anything!

*   *   *

Bright Sunshine greeted J next morning. Winter was on its way out, and spring was approaching. New leaves, wild breeze, clear blue sky, and lovely seasonal flowers had started to bring happiness all around. After breakfast and an hour's study, J rushed to the clubroom; he was dying to see his friends. But the room was locked from inside. Was it curfew time again? J wondered. Only during curfew time he and his friends used to lock the door from inside. But now there was no curfew. Then why his friends locked the door from inside? An impatient J began to knock on the door. Sona-da opened the door with an angry face, "What do you want? An important meeting is going on… go away… Your friends are not here", Sona-da slammed the door in front of J. Where were his friends? J could not see them anywhere. He went to the Pirbaba's Masjid, and heard whispers. He looked up. Dinka, Utpal and Gundi were seated in three different branches of the Mango tree. They looked like monkeys from below.

"Hey J, come up", Gundi said.

"But is he completely cured?" Utpal enquired, "Pox is contagious and dangerous".

"I bathed with turmeric yesterday" J shouted.

"What about the rashes, all gone?"

"Oh yes" defended J.

"Okay then, come up", Dinka said in a commanding tone.

J quickly climbed up and sat in a branch.

"You went to the clubroom?" Dinka asked.

"Yes",

"What did they say?"

"Sona-da looked angry"

"Yes they are having a serious meeting… all elders… elections are near". Dinka told with all seriousness.

"Hell with the meeting", Utpal said, "Sunday is for our Carrom matches".

We will go and play after the meeting", Dinka said in an optimistic voice.

"Hey what about the cricket matches?" J asked

"Our district lost all three"

"And Hapa?"

"His highest score was twelve in the last match… it is not a school game friend… it is not child's play… it is big cricket", Gundi said with proclaimed authority.

From the Mango tree, they kept an eye on the club room. The door opened once, and H'da went out quickly; and the door got closed again. After about ten minutes, H'da came back with a kettle, and many earthen pots.

"He went to buy tea", Gundi said.

"But when the meeting would be over"? Dinka asked impatiently.

"God knows", Utpal said in a Philosopher's voice.

"Hey is it a meeting of the Naxals?" J asked, "H'da is a Naxal we all know".

"Shhh... don't shout", Gundi whispered, "H'da, G'da and T'da are no more Naxals, they have joined the Confluence Party... The local Confluence leader is also inside... elections are near".

Kabir shouted from below, "you all are here? It is 1 p.m. already. Won't you go home?"

"Half an hour more, you also come up please", Utpal replied. Kabir climbed up and sat on J's branch. "Hey are you cured?" he asked.

"Yes completely", Gundi replied on behalf of J.

"You all must have come for carrom; but the meeting will continue", Kabir informed.

"This is an important meeting", Kabir continued after a pause, "H'da told me yesterday that Confluence would win this time because Priti G had won the war".

Kabir is close to H'da, they knew.

"How long will it continue", Dinka asked desperately. "May be up to 2 p.m.... 3 p.m.... 4 p.m...This is an important meeting", Kabir replied.

"Ah! this Sunday is gone", Utpal lamented.

"I would have surely defeated you in the carrom match today", Dinka told Gundi.

"Never, that would never happen; anyway, you may dream", Gundi replied dismissively.

"Today I was determined", Dinka said, "but for the meeting..."

"But for the meeting, you were saved from another defeat", Gundi joked.

"Don't boast, I'll surely defeat you someday", Dinka told.

"That Someday will never come", Gundi replied.

"But this day is gone" Utpal rued again. "Let's go home… hell with the meeting… hell with elections".

H da's predictions (as narrated by Kabir) came true. Confluence Party won the Assembly Elections in West Bengal. The English Daily wrote: "This victory was due to Priti's leadership capabilities that helped India to win the December War". J read the news item with utmost interest. Mr. K. S. Das became the Chief Minister of West Bengal. Youths of different localities in this town, many of whom were Naxals a year ago, now started to join the "Yuva Confluence" (Youth Confluence). The Yuva Confluence men gradually became associated with a unique dress code, not dictated by the party, but became a custom because everyone used to wear it: white pyjama, not too loose; and mostly white kurta with a round, little high collar over it. The ladies, as usual wore saris. The colour of the kurta for men often varied, -cream, saffron, yellow, sometimes green; -but the pyjama was always white. And in every locality, Yuva Confluence men became the bosses; -settling disputes, maintaining 'peace and order' in the locality, and becoming adjudicators and arbiters. Many of them also became 'contractors', -annexing contracts for building roads, bridges and other government projects through their connection with the political leadership. With heavy-sounding motorbikes, they roamed around the town.

Das was a tough administrator, and soon his government started to crack down on the Naxals. It was necessary to bring peace and rule of law to the state, opined many elders of the para like Niladri's and Utpal's fathers, Gundi's uncle, Kabir and Dinka's mothers, Barun's aunt etc. But due to the crackdown, many youths fled the town, and even the country, many died in 'encounters' with the police, many were reported as simply "missing". The reactions were mixed: families of policemen, whom the Naxals targeted as enemies, were happy; so were the businessmen, ordinary and rich; and the land owners, - little or big, and the 'peace loving' middle class. But families of young men and women, who were arrested and tortured for being Naxals, became annoyed and angry. Time rolled on. The state of Bengal embarked on a journey to the future.

Bhai surprised everybody in an autumn evening when he announced that Amit-da was reported 'missing' since long.

"But he was not arrested, at least we din't know", Fulda said.

"Nobody knows, where he is", Bhai reported, "his house is locked, his mother and sister have gone too".

"But where?" Chhordi enquired.

"I said nobody knows. There are two sets of gossip in the air, - first, they have all gone to Bombay, to their uncle's place; second, they were arrested and sent to prison in a different town".

"Sonali must be knowing", Anjali said.

"Nobody has seen Sonali for a long time also", Bhai told, "either she is indoors, or she has gone elsewhere. Her parents are tight-lipped now-a-days…"

There is an atmosphere of fear" Chhordi said.

"I heard that G'da and H'da informed police about Amit-da, and Police arrested him", J joined the discussion.

"You little Pundit", Fulda said, "don't ever utter these speculations outside. The time is not good".

"But Kabir told me secretly", J tried to be bold.

"Don't ever say this to anybody J", Barda told with concern, "these are all speculations. Nobody knows for sure… It is not a good time". There was something in Barda's voice that made J silent. He was not sure also. Amit-da was a hot issue among his friends now-a-days, and Kabir only told this to J the other day.

"Remember J, don't utter these words to anybody outside" Barda reminded, "time is not good". J nodded in approval.

"When is time good for this cursed state?" Ma murmured, "We have entered one unhappy period from another… from one set of fear to another… Oh God, when will this journey end?"

India's independence was celebrated with pomp and grandeur everywhere throughout this year. Several new patriotic songs, some very mind- boggling and catchy, had been composed by noted musicians. The All India Radio aired these songs frequently. These were also aired through microphones in every locality. Drama, seminars, talks, patriotic plays, competitions on singing patriotic songs, reciting poems, sit and draw for children, patriotic movies in the cinema halls, - all went throughout the year. J participated in recitations of patriotic poems, and won two prizes, -one first and one second. He also got a small 'part' in a patriotic play, organized by elders of the locality, and everyone praised his 'role'. He went to hear talks, and attended many cultural functions. Patriotism was everywhere, and the year was full of activity for Priti Gautam, K.S. Das, and J.

Ojha sir's class was always interesting because he went beyond the syllabus and discussed everything happening in the world outside the classroom. His classes used to be lively because he discussed society, politics, sports, films, besides History. Everybody in J's class, as also boys of senior classes liked Ojha sir and his classes very much. Even the 'bad boys' also loved and attended Ojha's class. Today, Ojha began the class by asking questions like:

"Do you know who the new Chief Minister of West Bengal is?"

J almost jumped up and answered, "K. S. Das'. J liked these questions from 'Current Affairs', a term he had learnt from Fulda and other elders.

"Very good. I knew you would be able to answer, because you read the newspaper regularly". "Who else in this class knew the answers, tell me honestly", Ojha sir asked. A few hands were raised, and sir looked pleased.

"This class is good and matured. That's why I discuss many things in this class", he commented.

"After the Assembly Elections, two things are noticeable, one good, one bad", he paused. J and his friends got very curious to know the good and the bad. But Ojha continued his silence. The boys got impatient and pleaded the teacher to continue.

"First I will talk about the good thing... the good thing is... a change has come... in a democracy change is required... people have voted a new government to power. This is good. But the bad thing is... people from other parties are now joining the Confluence..." Ojha paused and looked around, "These people always want to be close to power... these people are not good for any party", he continued, "when Confluence will be out of power... they will leave the Confluence party and join the party in power. These people are opportunists. They are harmful for any party".

J was thinking of the G'da's and H'da's in his para and thought that sir was right, but he remained silent because Barda and Fulda told him not to discuss these issues in public.

"You are too young to understand everything... but one thing you would understand easily... a person who changes colour frequently is not a human being... he is like a chameleon... kind of a lizard". The whole class laughed.

"And lizards will soon poison human beings and their noble parties"

Ojha sir always discussed 'forbidden' issues so casually, and made his class hugely attractive.

"I will tell you more when you are in the senior class... now I will tell you about Shah Jahan, the Mughal Emperor, who built...?",

Sir threw the question in the air. And the whole class shouted in chorus "Taj Mahal". Everybody, even the 'bad boys' knew that the famous Taj Mahal was built by Shah Jahan. "He could build it because he had a wife", Ojha sir joked, "I could not build one, because I do not have a wife". The class laughed again.

"Why don't you marry Sir", Paul asked.

"You search a bride for this fifty four year old man... try... if you succeed, you will be given double promotion". The class laughed again.

"Why didn't you marry earlier?" Banku asked.

"Because I could not find a Mumtaz... Shah Jahan got her earlier... but if you get good wives you can build several Taj Mahals", Ojha paused.

"Another Taj Mahal as exquisite as the existing one can never be built", Tapas said.

"That is right... you are absolutely right... then... then... you would build a new India... an exquisite India, better than the existing one... you can build it, with or without a wife... try to build a lovely India... an India where human beings won't live like lizards, they would live like proper human beings... head high in the air, not crawling on the ground... you will live in that India... probably I will be no more at that time", Ojha looked very serious and engrossed when he uttered these words.

J looked out of the window. A dark cloud was approaching the Sun. Would there be rain this afternoon, or would the clouds go away? Would the cloud cover the Sun fully? Would it be dark soon? Many probabilities appeared in J's mind. Did his father still hover in the cloud? And when it rained, did he fall on the earth with rain-drops, or go up to hide somewhere else in this vast sky, or float in the air in some other parts of the world? Did lizards also float in the air after death? Would Ojha sir also become a spirit after his death? Oh, everything was getting so confusing, so complex! Did spirits live eternally? Did human beings only become spirits after death? What about other animals? J would ask all these questions to Ojha sir one day. He wanted to know more about these mysteries. As Ojha sir concentrated on Shah Jahan, J was watching the movement of the clouds from the large window of the classroom.

8

ATOM BOMB AND THE FOUR ON SNOW

A new word has been added recently to J's notebook on English vocabulary: 'Exigency'. It means 'need of the hour'; kind of 'do it now', if the meaning is more simplified, J has learnt. The Government has declared National Exigency in India. Everybody should report to duty on time. No work should be delayed. No political meetings, protest movements, campaigns are allowed; and the right to freedom of speech and movement has been curtailed. J already heard a heated discussion in Sitaramda's shop over this 'Exigency' in an autumn evening when he went there with Barda to buy sugar:

"It is the right thing for this wrong country", Mr. Saha shouted, "Priti Gautam has done the right thing. Look, now everybody is attending office on time, buses and trains are running on time, no one dares to take bribe. This country must be handled authoritatively", Mr. Saha concluded.

"But look at other sides also", Mr. Sahoo, the Maths teacher responded, "press freedom has been curbed, opposition leaders are being harassed; is this a democratic country?" he asked.

"Hell with democracy. Where people are illiterate and corrupt, democracy is nothing but a big zero", Saha looked agitated. J, now in class VIII, knows that democracy means people's rule. He is curious to hear more about democracy in the debate.

"We want a responsible and good government, whether democratic or autocratic", Mr. Swamy commented.

"Oh, what a silly statement; how can an autocratic government be good"! Mr. Sahoo exclaimed.

"Swamy is right", Saha said, "in this country you need benevolent autocracy to crush corruption and misrule, and India's government is just doing that at this moment. In history you can find such Rules known as Benevolent Autocracy".

"Autocracy can never be benevolent", Sahoo said, "it is always dictatorial and harmful".

"Only Confluence Government can do better for this country", Saha opened up again, "and Priti is the most renowned and respected leader. Look at her records: victory in the December war, nationalization of banks, making India a very strong power by testing nuclear bombs, and now Exigency. I can tell you this Exigency will do immense good to India", Saha paused.

Yes, J can remember, he added 'Atom Bomb' to his 'vocabulary' Notebook last year.

"You are saying atom bomb is a good thing for this poor country where millions are starved? Shame on you", Sahoo ridiculed.

"Look, you have to be strong. India is living in a den of enemies like Pakistan and China. And you must be powerful to resist them. You Leftists did not say anything when China exploded atom bombs. You are hypocrites", Saha fired at Sahoo.

"Not a question of China or America, the question is that this country is poor, and it cannot afford atom bombs", Sahoo explained.

"You cannot sit idle because you are poor. You must try to be strong as well as rich; otherwise 'your China' and Pakistan will finish you", Saha ridiculed again.

"My China?", Sahoo wondered.

"Yes China is so dear to you all, the Leftists", Saha gave a banter.

"Your Mehra also offered olive branches to the Chinese and said Indians and Chinese are brothers".

"We admit that was not a right policy. That's why Priti has gone nuclear to treat China a lesson".

Oh! that war-cry again", Sahoo continued, although I don't like Tarachand, but I am reminded of one of his sayings: an eye for an eye will make the whole world blind".

"You Leftists do not like Tarachand, Banwari Lal, Priti G. Actually, you do not like India. You only like China", Saha pinched.

"That is your verdict, not everybody's", Sahoo replied in disgust. J was enjoying the debate immensely, and wished it continue.

"Ah, we were actually discussing Exigency", Sitaram, the grocer reminded.

"Everything is related", Saha said, "Priti is handling the country better than Banwari Lal".

"The future will only prove", Barda said.

"Yes, he is right, the future will only prove", Swamy agreed.

"Yes, Priti will create history, I am telling you today", Saha told proudly. "She is an angel sent to this country by God to revive its lost glory".

"Maa Durga", Sahoo joked.

"Yes, Maa Durga; even more", Saha countered, "but you Leftists, how do you utter Maa Durga? You don't believe in God?"

Meanwhile a boy from a nearby stall came with tea and earthen pots. He poured tea from an enamel Kettle in to each earthen pot and handed over to the debaters. He hesitated to give a 'pot' to J, but Sitaramda said "give him a pot. He drinks tea and he is also a member of our team". Now everybody laughed.

Mr. Swamy said "Give two pots each to Saha and Sahoo", they need hot tea to calm down

"I am always calm", Saha said

"The living Tarachand", Sahoo joked. Saha kept silent.

After a pause Sahoo said again, "Hope this living Tarachand gets a ticket in the next election".

"Ticket or no ticket, I will support Priti Gautam", Saha replied

"Don't lose again if you get a ticket", Barda said.

"If you all vote for me, I will win. But I know Sahoo will not vote for me", Saha commented.

"My vote, my preference… May be I cast my vote for you", Sahoo said.

"The Sun will rise in the West then" Saha replied.

"Okay, let's get up… its 9.30 p.m. already. I have to close", Sitaram announced. And everybody including J, prepared to leave, rather reluctantly.

*　*　*

"Bought Sugar"? Chhordi asked Barda as he and J entered after parking the bicycle.

"Sugar… Sugar… I mean sugar… oh, forgot totally, such a heated debate was going on…forgot totally… hey J, why didn't you remind me about Sugar?" Barda threw the question to J.

"I also forgot", J replied.

"Two pundits, one big, one small, joined the debate, and forgot everything", Mother ridiculed.

"I am going out again to bring sugar", Barda looked guilty.

"It is already 10 p.m., no shop is open now", Chhordi said.

"Okay, I will definitely bring it tomorrow", Barda said.

"You will have tea without sugar in the morning", Chhordi announced.

"Oh! I can't take that boiled water", Ma said in disgust, "what that little satan was doing? He also joined the seniors' discussion?"

"No, he was listening with all attention", Barda replied.

"What would he do listening to seniors' talks", Ma appeared dejected

"That way he learns many things", Barda pleaded

"And we miss our morning tea", Ma ridiculed again

"Okay, we will have tea without sugar in the morning. People say it is good for health", Barda said

"For your fault, I cannot have that tasteless boiled water in the morning", Ma replied, "I will go without tea"

"Okay, that's not bad only for a day", Barda said

"Nothing is bad when you commit mistakes, everything is bad when I do one", Ma was in the belligerent mood again

"No more argument, I am tired and going for a wash", Barda left the scene as Mother watched with anger

J also quickly went to the Kitchen. Peace, no war, was his plan for the night.

* * *

That night, J had a unique dream. India and China were fighting a war again, and there was a possibility that atom bombs might be used in the war. In a hilly border region between the two countries, four persons were standing in knee-deep snow: Priti G, Chenglei Yang, Tarachand, and J. Yang really looked like Gopal-da, J found out finally. Tarachand was pleading with folded hands to Priti G and Yang to stop the war:

"This may be a nuclear war if it continues", Tarachand said, "Please stop the war. Wars are no solutions. You can always discuss your problems and solve them"

"Yes, I also avoided a war with my mother this evening and restored peace in the family", J said all of a sudden like he often did in Ojha sir's class.

Tarachand laughed, and surprisingly both Priti and Yang joined him.

"Look at this innocent child", Tarachand, the peace lover said, "fresh and eager to learn. Millions of such innocent children will lose their lives in China and India if the war continues. Future of both these countries is dependent on these children...Therefore, I plead you to stop the war", he appealed again with folded hands.

And suddenly rains of flower started. Flowers of all colours and shades began to fall on snow, and soon dots of pink, red, violet, blue, yellow, orange, green, maroon, mauve and many other shades of flowers decorated the vast canvas of white snow. It was a tremendous sight, very charming, very scenic, extremely beautiful. Priti, J and Yang got mesmerized.

Now Tarachand said, "Each one of these flowers is a child from India and China. They are beautiful. They are praying to you to stop the war, and think of this world, and its children. They are all so beautiful and innocent".

Priti Gautam picked up a small blue flower and handed it over to J. J picked up an orange flower and handed it over to Priti. Tarachand gave a bunch of flowers each to Yang and Priti, and disappeared suddenly. The other three got puzzled, and began to search him. They searched and searched and searched. Finally J got tired and fell asleep.

When he woke up, he found Priti G, Chenglei Yang and Tarachand joining hands and having a close and lively conversation.

"Where were you?" J intervened and asked Tarachand, the peace lover, and preacher of non-violence.

"He suddenly disappeared", Priti said, "we toiled hard to search. Finally we found him".

"You need to work hard to find peace", Yang said.

"I got lost among flowers, among the children of earth; how that happened, I do not know" Tarachand said.

"After a long search, we finally found him surrounded by innumerable flowers", Yang began to reveal the mystery.

"When we tried to approach him, all flowers started to get up from snow and cover us. Soon we were completely submerged with flowers; we had the feeling that children were crawling all over us. The beautiful fragrance coming from their little bodies took us to a different world, - a soft, colourful and joyous world; we were told to do away with bad odours and harsh measures. We got our real senses back", Yang paused.

"And finally when the flowers crawled back to the snow again, we could open our eyes, and found Him in front", Priti completed the story.

"And now they decided to stop the war and restore peace", Tarachand told J with a big smile.

"That's great. My mother, my Barda, my whole family would be relieved because my Chhorda won't have to go to another war", J said.

"Yes, millions of families in China and India would be relieved today", Tarachand smiled.

"Now I will take leave of you and go back to my place", Tarachand said and vanished all of a sudden. All the flowers vanished along with him, and the whole horizon of snow looked very barren, lifeless and gloomy.

"We all want the flowers back", J, Priti and Yang shouted.

"Yes we want the flowers back", J shouted again as he felt a big jerk in his body.

"Wake up, don't shout, it is already seven in the morning", Chhordi gave him a jerk. The morning sun was peeping through the window. J saw Tarachand, the Great Soul, smiling in the sunshine. He whispered, and only J heard: "let peace and sunshine come through every window on earth".

9

MOONLIGHT SONATA

The year was eventful for J and the nation. J passed the Secondary School Certificate Examination with a first division, and opted to study History, Politics, Philosophy, Economics, besides Bengali and English,- compulsory subjects,- at the Higher Secondary level in the same school. Attraction of Ojha sir's History class, and Arun sir's Politics class (as mentioned repeatedly by senior students) encouraged J to stay in the same school. J wanted to study Biology instead of Economics, but that option was not available in the school, and in fact, in the whole district. From the Higher secondary level, streams were marked as 'Arts', 'Science', 'Commerce' almost everywhere in India, and one had to choose his or her stream. Biology was a 'Science' subject along with Physics, Chemistry, Mathematics, Statistics etc. A student opting for 'Arts' (or 'Humanities'), could not take Biology. The 'Science' stream was in great demand because students and their parents believed that 'Science' could offer good career prospects. 'Science' had a social status as well. It was generally believed that only good and meritorious students could handle science subjects.

This hugely attractive combination of career prospects and social status encouraged most of the students, good and bad, to opt for 'Science'. Almost all of J's friends went for 'Science', including some who would have done better in 'Arts' or 'Commerce'. But their parents pressurized them to opt for 'Science'.

J and some of his friends took up the issue with Ojha sir one day. With Ojha, students felt free to discuss and debate anything above and under the Sun.

"When will our higher secondary classes start, Sir?", Paul asked.

"I think from next Monday", Ojha replied and added, "All of you have taken up Science or Commerce, I presume?"

"J has opted for Arts", Banku said.

"That's really good, in fact unbelievable. Students with First Division marks do not generally take up Arts these days", Ojha said, "J broke the tradition; and opted to study under this poor fellow", Ojha beamed, "Have you taken History?"

"Yes Sir', J replied.

"What is your combination of Subjects?', Ojha asked. J told Ojha about his combination.

'Well, in any case, this school cannot offer you many options", Ojha told his boys.

"Why can't I study Biology with History and Politics?", J asked Ojha.

"Yes that flexibility should have been there", Ojha said, "but unfortunately, most schools in this part of India do not offer that flexibility".

"But why, sir" J wondered.

"There are many reasons. There are dearth in teaching staff, laboratory and library facilities, teachers' reluctance to take extra load, and above-all, age-old mindset".

"But why don't you try to change this?", J asked Ojha.

"I raised the issue in a few meetings, and was shouted down by my colleagues. You know majority matters everywhere. I agree that this flexibility must be there. But I am helpless". So J could not study Biology. But he liked all other 'Arts' subjects, except Economics.

However, flexibility was observed in the results of General Elections, - in both Parliamentary and State Assembly Elections. The First non-Confluence coalition government, headed by Palonji Sardesai, assumed office in New Delhi. In Calcutta, a coalition of Left and like-minded parties, known as "Left Unity (LU)" came to power. The Confluence Party lost both the elections, probably due to harsh measures taken during 'Exigency', as per reports of newspapers. Moti Barman, a communist leader belonging to the largest and strongest of the Left parties, became the new Chief Minister of West Bengal.

*   *   *

"Durga Puja would not be celebrated from next year", Utpal surprised everybody in the club-room. A 'doubles match' was going on at the carom board, and Utpal, who could not get a chance to play, exploded the bomb.

"Why?" Everybody asked in chorus.

"Because the communists are in government, and they do not believe in religion", Utpal said in a know-it-all manner

"All rubbish rumours. Let's concentrate on the game", Dinka said.

"You'll believe only next year, when my words will come true", Utpal sounded confident.

"Then why would the Puja be celebrated this year? They are already in power", Barun wondered.

"This year, they have little time to impose the ban. After consolidation, they will ban it from next year", Utpal said in a commanding tone.

"How do you know?" J asked.

"My uncle, who is a member of the party, has told me".

"Then what will happen to the innumerable persons associated with the Puja: the idol makers, the pandal workers, the drum beaters, the priests, the electrical workers, in fact all of us?", J wondered. "The government would compensate them", Utpal was unputdownable today. Now everybody appeared to accept Utpal's words.

Dinka had a last ditch effort to salvage Durga Puja:

"If they ban the Puja they will lose election".

"That would be decided after five years. By that time people would get accustomed", Utpal was devastating in his arguments.

"Don't like this game any longer. Stop it", Barun told in despair as Utpal smiled.

"Life is meaningless without Durga Puja", Aziz joined the discussion.

"Please continue the game", Dinka pleaded.

"I may join if Barun does not want to play", Utpal said.

"That's why you put a ban on the Puja?" Dinka ridiculed.

"I said you'd believe me next year", Utpal told in a Philosopher's voice.

"He may be right", Gundi joined, "I also heard a rumour in the market today."

"Okay, let's stop the game. I am not finding any interest." Dinka looked dejected, "Aziz is right. Life has no meaning without Durga Puja".

*   *   *

Arun sir's first Politics class is scheduled at 1.30 p.m. tomorrow. J is excited because he has heard that Arun Naskar is one of the best teachers in the Higher Secondary Arts. J likes the subject of Politics, probably due to his interests in 'current affairs'. Although the possibility of Durga Puja being banned by the government keeps him a bit worried, J is nevertheless excited about his new course. BB sir will take the first class tomorrow. It will be an Economics class. Ah, God! To begin the day with Economics is really painful. After Economics, there will be an English class and then tiffin time, and after tiffin, the Politics class.

J had come to school early. After all, it was the first day at the Higher Secondary level. The H.S. Section of the school looked very calm, very silent. J went upstairs. A 'Science' class was going on, and he saw many of his friends in the class through the glass portion of the door. Gradually Arts students came, many from different schools, some from outside the town. And at 11 a.m. BB sir entered to take the Economics class. J went to a corner in the last bench. BB sir introduced himself, and asked the names of all students one by one and then started his lessons on Economic Theory.

"You are T's brother, aren't you"? The boy seated next to him whispered.

He was referring to Bhai.

"Yes" J replied in a low voice.

"He is a tough guy. Nowadays everyone fears his gang. But you are lucky, you are his brother", the boy said.

J remained silent. Of late, unpleasant reports were coming about Bhai. He was seen in many shady areas of the town with local toughs, and he had become the ring leader of this group. Rumour was abuzz that they were engaged in antisocial activities. Last year, when Chhorda came on a long leave, Chhorda's friends complained to him about Bhai's gang. Chhorda came home infuriated, called Bhai and started to beat him mercilessly with his military belt.

"You come from a good family. But you have become the black sheep", Chhorda yelled

Everybody got startled.

Ma rushed in and asked, "What happened?"

"What happened? I will kill him; he is giving a bad name to the family. I have got shameful reports about his whereabouts, his misdeeds. He is the black sheep of the family... black sheep of the family", Chhorda continued to beat Bhai.

Bhai initially was too shocked to put up a resistance. But ultimately he managed to dodge Chhorda and run out of the house. He did not return that night. Everybody in the family waited, but Bhai did not come back. Days passed and rolled into weeks, Bhai did not return. Barda traced one of his friends, and enquired him of Bhai. He bluntly said that he did not know. Everybody in the family, including J, was worried. Finally after a week, Bhai came back.

Ma said "Where had you been?"

Bhai curtly replied, "That's none of your business."

"You don't speak to Ma in that tone of yours. Mend your ways, Bhai. Otherwise it will be too late. I am warning you", Barda jumped to Ma's defence.

Bhai sat in silence, looking blankly into space.

"Give me food, I am hungry", he told after a long silence.

"Nobody will give you food in this household. Get out. Ask for food from your rascal friends", Ma yelled.

"Fine, I am leaving", Bhai replied and got up to leave.

Chhordi pulled him to the kitchen as Ma grumbled. Chhordi took out a plate, put rice and vegetable curry and handed it to Bhai. Bhai ate in silence, and went out. Since then he rarely came home. Many rumour involving Bhai started spreading in the locality. Soon he had become a source of trouble for the family.

BB sir was teaching Economic Theory in a monotonous voice, and the boy next to him was inspecting J.

"I heard that you are a good student. But your brother...", the boy was trying to gauge J's reaction.

"Why are you talking?" BB sir scolded the boy, and J got immensely relieved. He was not feeling comfortable around his new neighbour in class.

"Don't talk inside the class"

"Sorry Sir", the boy said as BB went back to his lessons.

"I will talk to you after the class", the boy whispered. Immediately when the class ended, J rushed to the 'Science' class, to his old friends.

At 1.30 p.m. the tall and bespectacled Arun sir entered the classroom. J shifted himself to the Middle bench, by the side of a quiet-looking guy. Like BB Sir, and RN Sir, the English teacher, Arun Sir also introduced himself, and began to know the name of each student. But unlike two earlier teachers, he paused after hearing J's name.

"Such a brilliant result and yet you took up Arts. Very good. No pressure from your family to take up Science, I presume?" he asked.

"No Sir", J replied.

"That's unusual, but very good. I heard about you from other teachers, but now I know you. Study well my boy. I am here to help you". J instantly liked Arun sir as he realized why this teacher was so popular among students. Arun Naskar enquired about each student, and finally said, "I will not teach today. Let's have an *adda*".

"Sir at least tell us about reference books", a serious-looking guy requested.

"You will have enough time to know about reference books. Today only *adda*", the teacher said as the boy sat down unhappy. The only message that Arun sir gave in his *adda* session was that one must be aware about their state, their nation, and in fact about the whole world if they wanted to study politics.

Winter vacations are round the corner. Small, light-skinned potatoes, oranges, cauliflowers, peas, beans, tomatoes, cabbages have flooded the market. These are the signs of a prosperous winter.

It has been fifteen days since Bhai disappeared. Ma, Barda and the whole household were tensed, but helpless. Gradually with time, all in the family were somehow getting accustomed to his prolonged absence. Fulda had heard from the local people that these days he lived in the fringes of the town. Police was not involved, yet. Elders in the family apprehended that the Police would eventually find Bhai guilty of his antisocial deeds after tracing him.

Moti Barman's government had not yet announced any ban on Durga Puja. And according to Ojha sir, lizards were active again, and growing in number in the society.

Ojha sir called his "Old boys" (J and his friends from the 'Science' Stream) to a room during tiffin time one day and gave a piece of chocolate to each student for their 'success' in the secondary examination. When Ojha sir and old boys were together, a long *adda* was always inevitable.

"I seldom find you together, now. That's why I called you all today to this room", Sir said.

"How are you sir? We miss your class", Gagan said.

"How come? You all wanted to become scientists, didn't you?", Sir laughed.

"Not me sir", J reminded.

"That's true. He is my only beacon light now", Ojha joked again.

"Do you scientists keep track with developments in society, or are you only looking through the bioscope?" Ojha was at his usual self.

"It is Microscope sir, not bioscope", Avijit said.

"It is the same to a poor History teacher", Sir remarked.

"Let me ask you, like I used to in the junior class, who is the Prime Minister of India?"

Several voices replied, "Palonji Sardesai".

"And next the obvious question to follow, who is the Chief Minister of West Bengal?"

"Moti Barman", the chorus was stronger this time.

"Good, you are in class XI now, and you should know these names. Changes have come at the centre and at our province, and I believe, changes are always welcome", Sir said.

"Yes you always told us that way", Aziz replied.

"Can you remember, I told you five years ago, you were very junior then, that some people always change colour with the change of government?"

"Yes sir, I can distinctly remember", J told Ojha sir as H'da and G'da appeared in his mind. Some other boys also nodded.

"The same thing is happening now. Those who had deserted the Naxals to join the Confluence, are now joining the largest Communist Party, currently in power. Others who were never Naxals, and boasted of being 'Confluencemen', have already become Leftists", Ojha said.

"Everybody has a right to choose and join his party of preference", Gagan protested.

"You are right. But when this preference is largely manifested always with a change of power, you feel awkward. And that is happening again in this state", Ojha replied.

"And the tragedy is, every party gets exalted when its ranks swell, and the largest party in power is exalted now", Ojha paused.

"Every mass organization would want its membership increased", J said.

"That's true again, but if you build your house with cards, and not bricks, it will definitely crumble. These opportunists are like cards, they float in the air. They change colours like lizards", Ojha replied.

"But how do you know who is a brick and who is a card?", J argued.

"That is where leadership in a party matters. It is not difficult to separate bricks from cards", sir pointed out.

"Are you a Confluenceman sir, pained at people leaving your party?", Paul joked.

"I told you I am not a Rightist, not a Leftist, not a Centrist, I am a Humanist", sir replied.

"That is very vague", Gagan said, "You have to join a party".

"But why"? Ojha protested, "Can't I live decently, can't I work for society, for my country and people without joining a party?", Ojha looked serious. "At your age, when I was young, I used to think that those who joined political parties were different from others, because they had chosen an ideology. And I also joined a party", Sir said.

"Which party sir", Aziz enquired.

"But very soon I left the party, because I realized that those who joined parties were enchained by party dictates, good or bad, mostly bad. They lost broader vision to work for people, for humanity."

"But sir, without party, how would democracy survive?" the 'Politics' student in J enquired.

"Yes that is a question, and that is a dilemma also. Today's democracy is party-based democracy. And in the name of democracy parties are doing havoc, because lizards run the show in every party. I am telling you I am not against party or party-based democracy, but I am against opportunists, against lizards. They are not good for society. Those who are joining the largest party today, will desert the party again if there is a change in government", Ojha said.

"Your lizard theory is interesting to hear, but how would you prevent the lizards from joining the party", Gagan asked.

"Not only a theory my dear Gagan Sir, it is a stark reality. I know it is difficult to stop the lizards from changing parties", Ojha said, "But watch your rank and file, observe your cadres, look at their motives, that is the duty of the leaders, and they have also failed in their duties. They also reap benefit from activities of lizards. That's why parties are full of lizards and these lizards always try to gain with the change of government. Yet change is necessary, otherwise authoritarianism, abuse of power would reach the maximum height. Change is therefore welcome" Ojha stopped.

"Oh, sir, is this a political meeting?" Paul joked.

"Not a political, but an awareness meeting; a societal meeting to be exact", Ojha replied as the bell rang indicating the end of the tiffin hour. And old Boys departed for their respective classes.

Finally Christmas vacation arrived. This time of the year is rather pleasant. In the morning, J played cricket with friends under the soft winter sun. When evening came, J would sit beside Chhordi in the kitchen longing for that irresistible cup of hot tea. The warmth of the coal-oven reached him, soothing him to a comfortable feeling. The faint, weak moonlight crept in through the half-opened window. It made the woods behind the kitchen look uncanny, almost mysterious. Red tomatoes and white cauliflowers rolled around in the company of green peas and thin green beans on the kitchen floor. They were also enjoying the warmth of the kitchen in the cold, moonlit winter evening.

In one such winter evening right after the New Year, Bhai arrived, looking disheveled. He didn't speak a word and went straight into the kitchen looking for Chhordi. Fortunately Ma and Barda, were outside. Fulda was studying in a room, and Anjali, as usual, was out with her friends. Only Chhordi, J, and Pari were in the kitchen.

"Would you like a cup of tea?", Chhordi asked Bhai.

"Yes".

"First go to the Bathroom for a wash. I'll send hot water. You look very dirty".

Bhai went to the Bathroom obediently and came back in a while.

"You make us worry so much, Bhai. Look at J. He is younger to you and yet he is such a nice boy"

"I know, he is good", Bhai replied, "Give me tea in a bigger glass. I am thirsty and hungry".

"Why do you smoke so much? Your breath smells terrible", Chhordi said

Bhai smirked.

"Where had you been so long?", Pari asked "Rumours spread like wild fire in the locality."

"I am not answerable to you", Bhai replied indignantly.

"Ah, Pari, you are younger to him. Don't pester him with these questions now", Chhordi said.

Pari silently walked out.

"When will you finish cooking?", Bhai asked Chhordi.

"Why? Are you still hungry?" Chhordi enquired.

"Yes. I feel tired too".

"I normally finish cooking by 8.30. Have more tea. I'll give you some left over biscuits. Take some rest after that. I will call you at 8.30".

"No, I will sit here, I like this place", Bhai said.

"Okay. I would suggest that you take an early dinner, at 8. The elders won't come before 10".

"Okay, Give me warm linens also; I will sleep in the verandah".

"Why? Sleep in a room".

"No, Ma and Barda will sleep in two different rooms. I don't want any trouble or any shouting this evening", Bhai said.

"Can't they see you in the verandah?" Chhordi laughed.

"I will fully cover myself and sleep. You manage the rest", Bhai replied.

"How long will I manage, Bhai? How long will I cover up for you? Mend your ways. Come home. Come back to your family", Chhordi said affectionately.

"There you go again. At least stop for this evening. Don't you all get tired taking digs at me?", Bhai retorted.

"Fine. I won't say a thing. Sleep at the other end of the verandah, not near the entrance. Cover yourself fully. I will manage the rest", Chhordi assured.

"That's like a good girl", Bhai pulled chhordi's cheeks.

J, Pari and Bhai had an early dinner that evening - roti, daal and vegetable-curry. After dinner, J and Pari went to their rooms. Bhai went to the other end of the verandah for his makeshift 'bed', covering himself fully. Anjali came back at around 8.45, Ma 15 minutes later. Barda, everybody knew was in Sitaramda's shop. He wouldn't come before 9.30 p.m. Anjali, Maa, Fulda, Barda and Chhordi would have a late dinner. As per expectations, Barda came at around 9.30, and they all sat for dinner around 10 p.m. J was studying all through this time, but now he started feeling sleepy. When he went to his bed, he heard Chhordi recounting her tale of Bhai's return.

"Bhai has come back. He looked tired and I sent him off to sleep. I plead you not to tell him anything this evening. Whatever you have to say, for God's sake, say tomorrow", she said.

Barda listened to Chhordi and did not utter a single word. Ma, for a change, also kept quiet. Probably there was something in Chhordi's appeal. J also felt very relieved and contended in his bed. The warm quilt made him forget his winter woes and miseries of this crazy household. He soon entered the land of dream in his sleep.

* * *

In his dream, J heard whispers. People were running helter-skelter. Someone carried a dish. There were cries in the air for help. Someone was groaning. There was a small group around this person. But they did not know what to do. The groan became loud, someone rushed downstairs, then came up again. Someone brought a big bucket of water, splashed it on the groaning person. The whisper continued and became louder. It was a sickening nightmare and J woke up with a start. He needed a glass of water and looked around. Nobody was inside the room. Was he still dreaming? Where had all these people gone? Ma, Fulda, Chhordi... where were they? J heard the old clock tick in a nagging monotony. His head hurt from the intensity of his wretched dream. But he was no longer dreaming; he had woken up.

He found the door of the room wide open. Outside, at the far end of the verandah his siblings stood huddled in a group. They watched in disbelief as Bhai groaned and writhed on the floor. J rushed to his side. Bhai was still writhing in pain.

"When will Barda come back with the doctor? His condition is not good", Chhordi said looking alarmed.

J realized that Barda had gone out for the Doctor.

"Would he get any doctor at this time of the night?" Fulda whispered.

"What is the time now"? Chhordi asked.

"2 a.m" Fulda said.

Whitish froth had gathered at the corner of Bhai's lips. Tears rolled down from his eyes. Chhordi kept wiping his face with a wet cloth.

"You'll be fine. You'll be fine. Hold on a bit more. The Doctor will come soon. We are here. We all are here.", Chhordi sobbed silently holding on to Bhai

Bhai's groaning became louder. He wanted to say something. But his voice was low and his words were not clear.

"B---l----a----c----k, b----l------a------c------k, s-------h-------e--------e--------p", Bhai was taking unusually longer time to finish a word.

Barda arrived, looking defeated.

"No doctor", he said, "Knocked Dr. Sanyal's door for long. No answer. He must be removed to the hospital. I will call a rickshaw". Barda again rushed downstairs. Fulda and J followed him. Fulda forgot his spectacles, and he stumbled in the dark staircase. Barda told him to go back. J followed Barda to the road outside. Dim bulbs hanging from the lamp post amid moonlight greeted them. No Rickshaw was found on the road.

Barda asked, "Do you know how long is Haru, the Rickshaw Puller's home?"

"In the fringe area, outside the town", J replied.

"What will I do? How will I get a rickshaw so late in this winter night?" Barda asked in despair

Few stray dogs loitered around them, waving their tails. J and Barda were known faces to them. Barda went upstairs again, as J remained on the road with the dogs. He waited for a rickshaw to pass by! The moonlight was stronger now, unlike earlier in the evening. It almost blinded J in his helpless, desperate state. He didn't know what to do. Should he go upstairs to help Bhai? Or should he remain on the road in search of the elusive cycle-rickshaw? His common sense told him to remain on the road.

Barda returned breathless, "Found any rickshaw?"

"Not yet", J said.

"His condition is serious".

The landlady and her sons and daughters also came on the road.

"Can he be removed to the Hospital on bi-cycle?" The eldest son of the landlady asked.

"Not in his present condition.", Barda replied.

"Anybody has a phone in the locality?" the Landlady asked

"No, no one has a phone in our locality", J replied

Suddenly Chhordi's scream was heard. Barda quickly ran inside. J followed.

Bhai lay still on the floor. The groaning had stopped. He was not writhing any more.

"He has become still, do something please", Chhordi cried.

"Barda, let's take him on our shoulders", Landlady's son suggested.

"Is that possible? The Hospital is four kilo meters from here", Barda looked aghast

Bhai groaned and convulsed for one last time. And Moonlight watched it all with quiet smile. It spread across the leaves of the palm tree. It enshrouded Bhai's body in a silvery glow. J looked at Bhai, and at the palm tree. The tree was standing like a big strong dark demon with all its branches and leaves spreading like hundred dreaded arms toward the moon.

This was the moon that created ocean tides. This moon ignited the imaginations of several hundred romantics, ushered in poetry and music for generations, thought J. But this moonlight was watching his brother's deadly agony this night with its crooked but horribly silent smile.

"My brother must survive", J told himself as he hurried downstairs again for a cycle-rickshaw.

When he was about to step out of the door to the road, loud cries reverberated the air, - cries of ladies in the family, - Chhordi, Pari, Anjali. J rushed back

"Our Bhai is no more, our Bhai is no more. We lost our brother", Chhordi grasped J tightly, and howled like a hysteric. She was inconsolable. Ma looked shocked, as she sat in a corner. Barda was holding Bhai's wrists, trying to feel his pulse! A few neighbours assembled, all watching Bhai lying calmly on the verandah with moonlight all over his body and face. He ultimately surrendered to the ubiquitous moonlight after some abortive attempts at survival!

The doctor came at 7 a.m. in the morning and declared the 'patient' dead. He whispered to Barda to follow him downstairs. J also followed them quietly.

"He must have consumed lethal poison. Didn't you try to remove him to the hospital on time?" the doctor questioned. Barda remained silent in agony and anger.

"A post-mortem is required. I will write accordingly", the doctor advised.

"Post Mortem?" Barda asked.

"Yes. This is not a normal death. You don't want the involvement of the Police, do you?", the doctor said in a harsh voice.

Barda looked devastated, "Okay, whatever you think best".

"Try to go early. There are a lot of complex processes involved", the doctor suggested.

Barda came back upstairs after seeing the doctor off. Loud screams of ladies continued. Sankarda, Sitaramda, Mr. Saha, Mr. Sahoo and all seniors of the locality had already arrived. Barda called his friends to a corner and whispered something. They went downstairs. Then Barda called Ma and Chhordi. They were not in their normal condition. Barda whispered something again to them. Now they began to cry louder. Anjali, Pari and few of their friends joined. About half-an-hour later, Sankarda came back with a van-rickshaw. After sometime Bhai, wrapped in a white bed-cover, was laid on the van amidst uncontrollable cries. Barda and Sankarda sat on the two front corners of the van-rickshaw. Other elders would follow it on feet. Ladies and juniors, including J, were not allowed to follow. The van-rickshaw and its followers finally moved out, grim and silent, as neighbours assembled at their doors, windows and rooftops. J watched in pain another funeral procession, vastly different from the one he had seen several years ago.

10

MOTHERLAND

Life rolled on. Red star continued to smile and shed its light happily on Calcutta and Bengal as Moti Barman's Left Unity government completed five years. But the light of the star was not enough to brighten Bengal as prolonged power cuts crippled public life. Thank God, there was no stopping of Durga puja, or any other religious festival that Utpal's uncle predicted five years ago. Uncles did not know everything, - Moti Barman and his comrades proved. Team India meanwhile won the cricket world cup, and the nation went crazy. Big cut outs of cricketers were garlanded in every locality and decorated. Even *pujas* (worshipping) were performed for cricketers in many areas. Moonlit nights were not dark any more, they gradually became bright.

Life certainly rolled on. Ojha sir died of heart attack, two years after his retirement. Lizards crawled all over his body, mind, and probably, heart. With Ojha, idealism died a natural death; but unlike Ojha, it died expectedly, after prolonged illness. J graduated and took admission in post graduate class. Khalistan movement gathered momentum as a community of people wanted to secede from India for their own state.

Whose India is it? J sometimes wonders. Who cares about the hungry, poverty-stricken, defeated Indians? Do the fiery socialist, egalitarian, and the liberal leaders think of them? Do the angry rebel student leaders of J's university spare a thought for them? Does J care for them? They live in India, but they live outside India. J feels ashamed now-a-days, ashamed for the fact that 'progressive' 'educated' India fails to make India progressive in truest sense.

One day J told K, his room-mate at the university hostel that he wished to listen to the pavement-dwellers; he wished to spend nights with them on the footpath. K initially thought that J was joking. When he found out that J was serious, he tried to stop him. K was very close to a student leader at the university, a leader whose organization was thought to be sympathetic to the poor. J did not like the leader, his poise, his attitude, but he liked K. He wanted to know whether K was willing to come along. K was unsure, a bit cautious, and afraid.

"You speak for the poor and the wretched; why are you afraid to meet them?" J asked

"I am telling you a simple fact J, 'we' and 'they' are different", K sounded cautious

"I agree. We are educated, they are not. We can arrange a few meals, they cannot. We live 'here', they live 'there'. But have we ever tried to meet them?" J queried

"Don't be childish. Meeting them once in a lifetime cannot solve all their problems", K was forthright

"This is just the beginning, not once in a life time. I want to work for them. So I need to know them", J said

"Are you really serious?" K looked through J; "Many criminals and anti-socials are there among them. And if you wish to work for them join an NGO"

"I wish to work on my own, not through any NGO. And talking about criminals and anti-socials, can they be so poor?" J asked

"You should know that poverty leads to crime" K said, "many criminals live among them"

"How do you know?"

"This is common knowledge my dear reformer, everybody knows".

The conviction in K's words made J helpless and he decided that he would give more thoughts to his plan. "Well, I'll think about it, but I am not abandoning my plan", J said in despair.

"Leave your absurd plans behind. This can't materialize. Help the poor, but not the criminals. You will be watched by the police".

J took out a cigarette and left for the toilet. K sounded convincing and logical, he thought.

The next day the student leader called J to the canteen. "I heard from K your plan. It's splendid. I can accompany you. K is a nervous guy, you know. He will never go with you. I am ready to go. In fact I know many poor, many on the footpath".

J became very angry with K. Why on earth did he reveal his plan to the student leader?

"I can arrange many such people at a short notice. Then you, I and a few others from our organization can meet them. In fact, we can raise some money and give them when we meet them. In fact we have been thinking on these lines for some time", he said

Politics of poverty, J thought, but remained silent.

"I will fix a day and inform you. It's better to go in a group, rather than individually, and go to a known group, rather than any unknown poor or vagabond or criminal", the leader was in full command.

The leader ordered two cups of tea and said, "You deserve huge compliments for such a good idea. There are many enthusiastic persons in our organization, but not many have original ideas like you. That's why we need you in our organization".

"This is nothing great, nothing original. I just wanted to meet and spend time with my fellow countrymen", J said.

"You don't know how our meeting will create an impact among students. We are only confined within our university. This is the chance to spread to society, chance to help the poor. I am thinking about taking a photographer with us. He will take pictures when we would hand over money to the poor, and we will print those pictures in our newsletter and distribute among students. It will create a huge impact, and many would be drawn to our organization. Don't you like the Idea? But keep it a secret. The rival organization always implements our plans".

Poverty of politics, J thought, but remained silent. Meanwhile the leader's girlfriend arrived, - a glamorous, beautiful lady from an affluent family. J always admired her. He secretly wished that she talked to him. But she was always oblivious to J's presence. J was neither handsome, nor smart. Moreover, he had a small town look. J envied the student leader.

The lady cast a glance at J, probably for the first time, and then she looked at the leader.

"Okay, I will inform you about the time. Be prepared. Good plan", the leader told J before leaving with the lady.

*   *   *

"What were you doing with that hypocrite, that fraud?" N, the leader of the rival student body arrived with his followers as J was leaving the canteen.

"You are such a nice guy, don't fall prey to his gimmicks. It's all lie and rubbish", N put his hand on J's shoulders in order to make J sit again. J realized that N and his friends had been watching J and the student leader from the other end of the canteen.

"Come, let's talk. You should know the truth. After all you are new to this university", N and his followers sat around a table, and pulled J to sit with them.

The canteen-boy served tea and 'singara'. J was feeling a bit uncomfortable. He wished he could leave, but that seemed impossible.

"We are what we are, we are not hypocrites. We don't cheat students with false and lofty ideas". Did they hear J's conversation with the student leader? Why was N referring to lofty ideas? Someone from their group must have heard their conversation. But no one besides him and the student leader was around when they were talking! J tried to remember. The canteen-boy came twice, to serve tea and to collect the cups later. The girlfriend came at the end of their conversation. Did the canteen-boy pass on any information? But he spent a few seconds in their table, and remained busy with his work. It was impossible for him to guess anything.

"You have seen for yourself the pro-poor guy, who sheds tears for the wretched man on the street, went away with the most beautiful and affluent lady of our university", N looked at his followers as they gave a despising smile.

"A hypocrite to the core. What was he telling you? Coercing you to join his organization?"

"He doesn't coerce, his methods are different, he persuades with silk and butter", one of N's followers said as others burst into loud laughter

"That's why he is so dangerous", N replied, "Never trust that man. In fact he and his organization have done nothing for the students, nothing for this university. You know, only three years ago a large number of students of your department failed in the final examination. We forced the authorities to clear them. Imagine the plight of a student who fails at the final examination. Think of yourself, studying at this university for two years and then failing at the final exam. What would happen to you, to your career? At that moment of despair, if we don't stand beside you, what would you do? Can you fight for yourself alone? You can't. But we are always by your side. We are always by the side of the students. They talk big, they talk about the society, about the poor, but they are never by the side of the students, by the side of the poor either", N took a pause.

Did he hear their conversation? Suspicion grew stronger in J.

"We don't talk big, but we act. And we act for the students", N resumed, "Have you gone to the Boys' Common Room?"

J nodded in affirmation.

"Who brought the Table Tennis Board there? Who made the toilet there? We pressurized the authorities to create these facilities for the students". N said

"But there are also girls among students. I heard they don't have a separate common room", J said.

"You are absolutely right. Now we are fighting for a Girls' Common Room. A big room with toilet, where girls can relax"

"But why not a TT Board for them as well?" J asked

"You are right. Although they seldom play, we should also demand a TT Board for them as well. Hey S, include that in our list of demands to the authorities". S nodded quickly.

"Look out for us, we will make a Girls' Common Room very soon. After all, we think for the students. If you join our organization, you are not alone. Just tell us your demands. We will get it done by pressurizing the Authorities".

"Tell him about last year's episode", one of N's followers reminded

"Which episode?" N asked

"The Gherao"

"Oh, that was a real victory for the students, for our organization. You know, in the Biology Department, the Authorities did not allow more than half of the students to sit for the examination due to lack of adequate attendance. We started an agitation, talked to the Authorities, but they did not relent initially. Then we gheraoed the Authorities for 48 hours, and they finally relented and agreed".

"Agreed to what?" J asked

"They allowed all to sit for the exam. Such is our commitment towards the students. We are always by their side", N looked very proud.

"What is the minimum attendance required for sitting at the exam?" J asked

"Officially sixty per cent, but unofficially, nothing", one of the followers said

"Look, at this age you may have many things to do - Part-time jobs, tuitions. You might want to go for a movie or a drink with friends. Moreover, you may be ill, you may be in a bad mood, and you may have union activities. They don't understand. It becomes almost impossible to maintain minimum attendance", N clarified as J heard him attentively.

"I heard that you hail from a small town. Things might have been different in the degree college of your town. But here in this big city, everybody is busy; everybody has different engagements, very little time to attend lectures"

"Then why enroll in a university?" J queried

"That's the big question everybody asks, from professors, to guardians, to students like you", N is now fully engrossed in the issue.

"What to do without joining a university? You don't get jobs after your bachelor's degree. I bet half of the students would not study further had they found jobs after graduation. Here at the university, you get more degree, like the Masters degree, and you can spend time as well", N laughed, and his followers joined.

"But how can I get my Masters degree without attending classes?" J was curious.

"You will learn the trick my dear, you will learn it gradually. But for any problem, we are here", N said with an air of confidence.

"This boss will solve all your problems at the university", a follower pointed to N as he took a singara from the plate.

"Join us. I like small-town guys like you. There are many in our organization. They are gentle, intelligent and straight. Vote for us during elections, we will always be by your side. Don't be misled by hypocrites, you won't find them during crisis", N advised.

"We normally sit at the Common Room. You will find us there from 12 noon to 4 p.m. Come you will like our company", a follower informed

"Hope to see you on Monday, for now bye my dear fresher", N said while leaving with his gang.

J heaved a sigh of relief, not because the gang had left, but due to the fact that they did not hear his conversation with the rival student leader.

J was not unfamiliar with student politics. It was also there in his college. But here at this university, rivalry seemed intense, and the leaders talked more confidently, in more matured manner, like the leaders of mainstream politics. They were more persuasive, smart, and probably more clever than the student leaders of his college. J did not join student politics at his college; here also he would try to stay away if he could. He hailed from a poor family. He needed attendance, not attention, J thought as he started walking back to his hostel.

Khalistan movement for separate statehood gathered more steam. The leadership of the movement was gradually slipping out of the hands of the moderates, and extremists were taking control. In recent times an angry and extremist supporter of the Khalistan cause was emerging as the top leader. Government of India was disturbed with the extremist turn of the movement. But in Bengal, peace prevailed amidst long power cuts (popularly known as load-shedding), joblessness, and growing population. The LU government concentrated on land reforms in rural areas, a policy that seemed to yield good results initially. Italy won the football world cup last year defeating West Germany 3-1, although India continued to be obsessed with cricket.

Back at home, Chhordi got married to a middle-aged man who had no substantial income. He used to run a tea-shop near J's school in his home town. But the shop was nearing a closure, because the owner was reluctant to run this 'small business'. Meanwhile Chhordi got a job in a primary school, 150 km away from the town. She began waking up at 4.30 in the morning, prepared morning tea and lunch for her husband, and left for the bus depot on her way to school. It took three and half hours by bus to reach the school. Her job actually paved the way for her marriage. Otherwise, this 'ugly ghost' of a woman, would have remained unmarried. J's entire family considered her lucky for getting married. So Chhordi left no stone unturned to please her husband.

Life moved on as J continued to attend classes. Student leaders gradually stopped talking to J and he started to avoid them as well. He found many lectures boring, absolutely boring, but made it a habit to attend. He could not afford to skip classes. He was lucky to get higher education, which many of his brothers and sisters could not afford. A few 'irrational', 'non-progressive', 'insensitive' 'reactionary' students like him did not join politics, and instead chose to attend classes. Meanwhile the student leader and his followers went to meet the poor, gave them money and clothes, and photographed their activities. J did not accompany them. He communicated to the leader through K that he was not ready to go. The photographs earned many new members to the organization. The leader was very happy.

But J was not at all happy. Some unknown force from inside was urging him to go to the pavements, to know the plight of the people, to interact with them. J decided to request K again to accompany him. However, after many thoughts he decided to go alone. He wanted to face reality, not escape from it. After about a year from his initial plan, J went to the Downtown area in one Saturday evening, planning to spend two nights on the footpath, with pavement-dwellers.

It was late evening, around 11.30 p.m. J saw men and women preparing their 'beds' on the pavement, - tattered plastic sheets, and rolled clothes as 'pillows'. J also had a plastic sheet in the bag hanging from his shoulder. He saw people in the pavement sleep on these sheets. It rained in early evening. The road was shining under bright lights, shining like long black hairs of the proverbial Indian lady after a good long bath. Thankfully 'load-shedding', which rendered the city dark since early evening, was over. The road seemed very wide now, with little traffic, and few people. J watched men and women on the pavement from a distance. There could be criminals among them. He must be careful. Were the policemen also watching him? He looked around, but found no one suspicious. He lit a cigarette to fight nervousness, and continued to watch people. A family with two children had already gone to sleep. Close by, a boy was preparing his bed. Beside the boy, there was a gap, an entrance to a building, left unoccupied. After the gap two ladies, probably beggars, slept. Then there was another family. J found no one suitable to talk to. Meanwhile his cigarette was finished. A police-jeep sped past the area. J started walking. Everywhere people could be found on the pavement, jostling for space to sleep. After about 15 minutes of walk J found a man, with long beard, sitting at a corner of the pavement, looking vaguely at the road in front, - big eyes, curly hairs, but unlike a criminal. Finally J found his man and approached him.

At first the man did not notice J, he was sitting there with no purpose, not even preparing his bed; it seemed he could sit there for ages. J slowly sat beside him and offered him a cigarette. The man looked at J, and took the cigarette hesitantly. J took out his lighter and gave it to the man. He returned it, not willing to light the cigarette now; he placed it over his right ear. J took out a cigarette for himself as well, but hurriedly put it inside his bag.

"Hello, I am J, I wish to talk to you", J said in broken Hindi.

The man again looked at J, more piercingly this time, and slowly said "I speak Bengali".

"Oh that's a great relief, my Hindi is not good at all".

"But I speak Bengali", the man said sternly.

J became a little nervous. Had he chosen the wrong person? This person seemed a tough guy.

"Yes, yes, we can talk in Bengali" J said in haste.

"Are you a Reporter?" the man asked.

"No... Why?" J was at a loss.

"Reporters from Newspapers come here; they are like you. They talk to us, sometimes take photos".

"Have your photograph been published in a Newspaper?" J asked.

"I saw once. But it was in a group. I was at the rear end, hardly visible", the man was eager to describe.

"What did the reporter ask you at that time?"

"It was election time. He was doing a story on pavement-dwellers, as he told us. Whether the government has done anything for us, what do we think about the government, which party would likely to win elections, and why."

"Did you read the story later?"

The man remained silent. J felt a bit awkward.

"I can't read", the man said in a low voice.

J felt embarrassed now. He should not have asked this question.

"I am sorry", he said

"So you are not a reporter. Then why have you come here?" the man asked.

J did not know what to say, but he told the truth: "I am a student at the university. I am doing sort of a survey on people like you. I want to know what you think about our country, about us…I mean the educated people. I also want to know about your plight. I wish to get to know you better".

The man looked at J, with surprise. Slowly he took out the cigarette from the top of his ear, a match box from his pant, and lit the cigarette. He took a long puff, and slowly released the smoke. J did not talk either. After a few puffs, the man said,

"Where is your cigarette?" J was looking so intensely at the man that he forgot his cigarette. Now he took out the cigarette from his bag and lit it.

"Won't you sleep?" J wanted to strike off a conversation.

"Not the right time for me to sleep".

"It's almost 12. When do you sleep?"

"Around 2 or 3 a.m. Sometimes I don't sleep".

"How do you work at day time then?"

"I don't work regularly, sometimes I do".

"What do you do?"

"I work as a porter".

"At the train station?" J asked.

"No, they call me to different factories, to carry goods to the factory from the truck or to load goods in trucks. But I don't get calls regularly".

"How do you survive then?"

"Why? I earn".

"But not regularly?"

"Do you study regularly?", the man asked J, and J replied in the negative.

"Are you not educated then?" The logic is simple, but strong, J realized.

"If you don't mind, how much do you get in your work?"

"Depends on how much work is there, how much load I can carry. But you are not writing anything. What sort of an interview is it? Reporters always write".

"I said I am not a Reporter".

"But if you don't write, you'll forget. If you forget, you can never recall our conversation. Your study would remain incomplete".

J was astonished. The man was more intelligent than he appeared to be. J took out a small writing pad and a pen from his bag. The man appeared contended. At last, the conversation took the form of an interview. The man was after all used to interviews by Reporters.

"What do you do when you don't have work?" J asked.

"I roam about in the city. I watch people".

"How do you manage a meal when you don't have work?"

"I try to save for bad days. But if I don't have money I skip meals".

"A man carrying load, skipping meals…don't you feel weak?"

"What do to? It has become a habit. But to tell you the truth, I seldom miss my meal. I manage at least something. At least, some 'chhatu' and onion".

"Can your neighbours here manage regular meals?"

"I don't know. They come in the evening for sleep. Leave early in the morning".

"They come to this place regularly?"

"Yes they have booked this place".

"Booked this place?" J wondered.

"Yes we have to pay to the police and the local toughs for sleeping here".

"Really?" J was more than shocked.

"That is very common in this city. But we are asked not to reveal this to anybody, especially to Reporters. Anyway, how do I know that you are not a Reporter?"

"You can trust me. I have some papers from the university".

"I can't read. But you look like a good man. But don't reveal this to anybody. Otherwise I will be thrown out of this place".

"I won't. How much you have to pay?"

"Leave this issue, say something different. People concerned are watching".

J looked around, but saw nobody.

"They are sleeping at a distance. I mean not really sleeping." the man laughed.

"Won't they suspect you for talking to a stranger?"

"They may, they may not. I am a veteran in this pavement. I have met Reporters before".

"Can I spend the night here with you, can I sleep here?"

"That's impossible. The rule says no stranger can sleep here".

"The Rule?" J asked sharply.

"That's the rule here", the man said nonchalantly.

Rules may not always be written, J learnt from his books on British Constitution.

"Let's go for a cup of tea", the man proposed.

"Tea? At this hour" J wondered.

"Everything is possible at this place. I suppose you have money".

"Yes, some."

"Let's go. Tea always helps conversation", the man stood up and started walking. J followed.

The tea stall was a place bustling with activity and sound. A middle aged man was at the helm, and a boy was serving tea in earthen pots to the customers. The customers were all men, like J and his friend from the pavement; men of different ages, chatting in different languages, mostly Hindi and Bangla. But one could also hear Bhojpuri or Oriya. It was summer time. Men were mostly in 'Lungis', with the upper part of the body uncovered. The man sat on a block of stone near the tea stall and ordered two cups of tea. He seemed a known face to the stall owner and many customers. Some looked strangely at J standing near the block of stone, while some others remained busy in gossip. J did not like the place, it was impossible to carry on his 'interview' here; but he liked the tea. It was good. The man was sipping his tea in great satisfaction, and talking to his acquaintances. J saw one person offering 'biri' to the man and they started smoking. J felt a huge urge for smoking, and searched for his packet of cigarettes in the bag, but somehow resisted his urge. Cigarettes were out of place in this world of biris. He wished he had a packet of biri, he wished someone offer him a biri, but no one was paying any attention to him now, not even his 'friend'. The man was busy chatting with some of the customers. J walked a few steps, and looked at the sky. The usual hazy darkness descended. Were there any stars in the sky? J tried to search, but could not find any. Stars were hardly visible in this city-sky due to a hazy and smoky atmosphere above. J started missing the night-sky of his home town, and the bright twinkling stars. He remembered how he sometimes searched his father among the stars in his childhood days, particularly when he was in a crisis, when he required support, but his father was always absent, he was always dead, always invisible. He was never in the clouds, nor among the stars. His wooden chair vanished into perpetual oblivion. J stopped searching his father among stars when he was in college. He gradually realized that not everyone had a father to rely upon in this world.

The man finally finished his tea and gossip. He came to J and told him to pay. J followed his instructions obediently. The man bid goodbye to his friends and started walking with J. He asked for a cigarette from J. This made J happy. Now he could also smoke. They lit their cigarettes and started walking. The roads appeared emptier now; the city had gone to sleep, and J was walking; why he did not know. Was he walking with this unknown fellow for social commitment, or for ego-satisfaction? J did not know. But he was enjoying this walk, enjoying the unfolding new look of the city, enjoying his cigarette.

"Where are we heading to?" the man asked J.

"Don't know".

"Sorry for wasting your time at the tea stall. We can start again. But won't you go back home?"

"I stay in a hostel, and in no hurry to go back. Besides I told you I decided to spend the night on the pavement".

"Fine. Then we can go to the river side. You know it is close by".

"Won't you sleep?" J asked.

"I would also skip my slip this night".

"So we are heading to the river side?"

"Yes you get fresh air there, and fresh energy" the man laughed.

The river-side was desolate. A few beggars were sleeping on the benches built by the corporation. It was summer time and chances of rain had forced most of the beggars and vagabonds to look for covered pavements. But here, by the side of the river, there was hardly any covered area. J and the man sat on an empty bench under a palm tree. A cold breeze was blowing. J liked the area. He could talk through the night, in this calm environment. J started interacting again with the man. Gradually J came to know that the man also wanted to be rich. Although he remained poor always, he did not nurture any hatred for the rich. God had given him this life. The rich, he believed, must have done some good work in their past lives. Moreover, the rich were educated, hard working and hence successful in this life. He was not averse to the educated class either. "You need to work very hard for your education, you need to study a lot of fat books", he said. "Not everybody is capable of doing that much of hard work", he observed. When J pointed out that not everybody got opportunities in this country to go to school, the man remained silent for a while. Then he said that in his village he saw many boys from affluent families dropping out of school, because they didn't love to study. "In spite of getting opportunity and support to study in school, I have seen many boys in my village idle away", he said. "It is not easy to regularly go to school, flip through fat books and end up properly educated", he concluded. "But did you get any access to education?" J asked. The man remained silent again. After a long pause he said that he did not get any chance to go to school. "Aren't you angry for this missed chance?" J said. "No", the man replied and continued that he could also have dropped out of school had he got a chance. "Many among you could also continue" J reasoned. "I am not sure, really. To be properly educated is not easy, to continue in school is not easy, to study large fat books is not easy either", the man repeated his words. That's why he respected educated men like J. He admired them; they were intelligent, sincere and dedicated. God had given them these special traits in life. "Then God must be partial" J laughed, "He had given some of us these traits, and robbed many others of such qualities". The man bit his tongue and shook his head vigourously, in embarrassment and disapproval. "Don't say things like these. The Almighty cannot be partial. He has charted a course for everybody in this life. Not everybody deserves everything and God knows who deserves what".

"Then you think that you don't deserve money or education because the God does not want you to get these?" J shouted loud.

"Perfectly", the man confessed.

"Then why do you wish to be rich? You know that God doesn't think that you deserve to be rich", J argued.

"I am doing my duty. And God wants everybody to do his duty. If he is satisfied by anybody's work, he changes his fortunes; he makes him rich. You can see many uneducated poor persons also got rich through hard work. If I work hard, I may be rich one day", the man pointed out.

"You can never be rich, you know. Stop fooling yourself. God is always partial. He will never bestow wealth on you, idiot", J shouted angrily, in an unusual manner.

Bewildered, the man looked at J and remained silent, with his head down. The river in front appeared to be flowing into the darkness of oblivion. Dim lights blinked from the other side of the river. J lit a cigarette.

Was the man hurt? But when would these people realize their plight and rise up? Why had they accepted their suffering as part of their destiny? If the river in front could provide any answer; if the gentle breeze around could foretell, J wondered!

"Are you hurt?" J asked in a low voice, "I should not have shouted like that. I am sorry"

The man sat silently for a while. Then he suddenly stood up and started walking back, probably to the tea-stall area.

"Please don't mind. I said I am sorry", J sounded apologetic.

The man stopped, looked around and said angrily: "You call me an idiot? You yourself are a fool, a complete idiot. I would have punched anybody on the face if he dared to call me a fool or shouted at me…Because it was you, I remained silent…you provided tea, cigarettes…besides you are educated…but now I know that educated persons are also very impatient and arrogant". His rage took J by surprise.

"We work hard. We try to earn our meal…yes, we are illiterates, but that does not mean that one would malign us in this manner", the man continued, "We don't depend on you, the educated rascals, for our livelihood".

J remained silent. Let the man vent out his anger.

"To be rich and educated is not everything. You must learn to respect human beings. Don't treat them like dogs. Don't treat us, poor people, like dogs. You won't get any respect from us. We will also call you dogs, fools, idiots…"

"Calm down. I said I am sorry. Please come and sit down", J said in a low voice.

The man increased his pace of walking.

J ran a few steps in order to keep pace with the man. Suddenly J came in front of the man and kneeled before him. J touched his head on the road before the man with a view to prevent him from leaving. The man got bewildered, a bit amazed as he tried to make J stand up again. Two policemen on night petrol, J saw, were watching them from the other end of the road.

"How many bottles, my dear? Good drama, but wrong time", one of them shouted.

The man also looked back, and told J in a hurried but low voice: "Give them some money and cigarettes; otherwise we will be in trouble". J searched his pocket and found many coins. He also took out four cigarettes from the packet and passed these on to the man. The policemen came to this side of the road. "What are you up to at this time of the night?" one of them said in a harsh voice. "We are here for some cool fresh air sir. It's very hot there", the man pointed towards the central area of the city. "Good very good, come we will give you more fresh air", the policeman ridiculed. "We are not thieves sir, not criminals. We two are friends" J said. "All thieves and criminals are friends of one another", the policeman was quick in his reply, "anyway why are you here at the dead of night?"

"Just roaming about, no bad intention" J said.

"This boy looks like a student, but why are you with this man? It is a very unusual combination" the other policeman said.

"We are friends sir, indeed we are friends", J replied.

"Where do you study?" J mentioned the name of his university.

"Show me your identity card".

J had no identity card, but he had some papers from the university, and he showed these to the policeman. The policeman was not impressed. "Show me the real identity card of the university with your photo on it. I think your university provides these to students". "Yes, but.. but.. I don't have the Card right now", J said hesitantly. Meanwhile the man offered cigarette to the other policeman. Reluctantly, he accepted the cigarette. The man now offered cigarette to the person checking J's papers. "I don't smoke", he said sternly. The man brought out the coins now and handed these over to the policeman. "What do you think? Are we beggars, vagabonds like you?" the policeman threw the coins on the road. "Come to our jeep. You will have lots of fresh and sweet air for the remaining night; and for many more nights ahead".

J's 'friend' got busy searching and collecting coins from the road, as the two policemen were watching him. Meanwhile, J frantically searched and found two fifty rupee notes among many papers in his bag. He felt relieved and confident. "Pardon him sir; he could not understand your stature. I have something more for you". He showed the notes to the policemen. One of them snatched the notes from J and said, "Good to see that you have some sense, unlike that rascal". J gave a benign smile. "Okay, leaving you for the moment. But don't create any nuisance. Don't try to be smart. Go and sit there like good boys", the policeman pointed towards the empty bench where J and the man were seated a little while ago. J nodded in approval and said, "Don't worry sir, we will sit there". "Remember, don't try any mischief, or else you will be picked up". "Don't worry sir, I'll take care", J said politely. The two policemen left in their jeep as J heaved a sigh of relief.

The man collected all coins from the road and came back. He seemed relieved too. "You handled the situation very deftly. You are really intelligent" he said. J laughed, lit a cigarette and offered one to the man. He accepted it gleefully; he was no longer angry. They went back to their bench under the palm tree. The river and the breeze were flowing, uninterrupted by the power of the police.

J learned that night that the man voted in several elections, but he did not know about his actual age. "Around forty", he told J about his age. He knew that there was a Government in Delhi, but did not know how it was formed. He heard the name of Priti G, but did not know whether she was the Prime Minister or the President of India. He was unsure about the difference between 'Delhi government' and 'the government here', yet he voted for both Parliamentary and State Assembly elections. His voting preferences were largely determined by local toughs who controlled 'pavement allocation'. Before elections, they issued whips to pavement dwellers about which party or coalition they would vote for. Anyone violating the whip would be evicted from the pavement, and would face a lot of trouble in daily life. Therefore, nobody dared to ignore the whip. But in any case, the man always liked to vote. He felt that he was a very important person on any election day. Although his life had not changed for casting votes in the election. But he decided to vote in all elections; not because of any compulsion, but due to the fact that he loved to cast his vote. The 'vote babu' (polling officer) politely asked him to mark his finger print on the ballot paper in a secret surrounded area of the room where voting was taking place. In a few elections, members of political parties gave them money to go to the polling station by rickshaw, although they walked up to the polling station, saving the little money offered to them. But in one election, he was in trouble, caught between two fighting groups of rival political parties. He somehow managed to escape, but one pavement dweller died due to bombing. Despite everything, he always loved to vote. Strength of democracy in India? J was wondering. The man also talked about his family, his children, and how determined he was about educating his children. The government had made school education free in his state now, and both his children were going to school. But he was not sure how long his children would continue in school; they didn't like to study. He told his wife and parents living in his village to see that they continued, but he was still not sure. He had to come to this city for manual work, but he wanted to ensure that his children were properly educated and lived decently. He respected educated persons like J, but he had no grudge against anybody, not only the educated and the rich. Everybody was living a life God wanted him or her to live. He was a firm believer in God. The Almighty would also give him good days if he worked hard. Educated and the rich always worked hard for this life, and they got it. Those who inherited property were reaping on the hard work done by their forefathers. They were lucky, and the poor were unlucky, but you could change your luck, although it was mostly predetermined. J listened silently this time without any protest. J did not know whether lucks were changeable. But he realized that beliefs were hardly changeable. He thought that he could talk to more poor and illiterate people before coming to any conclusion. J came back to his hostel in early morning. Before departing, he offered all coins to the man. He refused to take these initially, instead wanted two cigarettes from J. But when J reasoned that the coins were logically his, because he picked these from the road with toil, the man accepted the coins. The man possessed self-dignity, J realized.

J fell asleep after reaching hostel. When he woke up at 1 pm, K, his room-mate, had already left for the university. J did not feel like going to the university, although two of his favourite professors would take classes in the afternoon. J took a long bath, and went to the 'dining hall' for lunch. Rice, daal, vegetable curry and a small piece of fish were served for lunch. Although the 'daal' was nothing better than water, J took it fully today, unlike other days. He thanked God that he was getting regular meals, which many of his fellow countrymen did not get. He decided to continue his 'survey', not by spending nights on the pavement, but according to his convenient time, like at noon or evenings on holidays, and late evenings on days when he would have classes at the university.

In the next few months J talked to more than hundred poor and illiterate persons, - beggars, rickshaw pullers, rag pickers, small tea-shop vendors, hawkers and others. He took papers and pens for all 'interviews', which gradually became more structured. His classes were not disturbed, because he went according to his plan. He gradually liked his 'work'; he could feel what his countrymen were thinking about different issues. Although J could not change their condition, he could try to understand their views. J felt happy with his job. As expected, J's respondents differed widely on many issues, held divergent opinions, expressed contradictory feelings, but J could also find some common areas in their views. At the end, J wrote down the findings of his survey in a long notebook, hardbound. He captioned it, VIEWS OF INDIAN POOR (and the illiterate) ABOUT MOTHERLAND. He summarized his findings numerically:

1. Majority of the Indian poor are jealous, but not angry about the rich or the middle class;

2. Some Respondents believe that the rich should be robbed of their wealth and equal distribution of wealth should be made. However they are unsure of the ways this could be done;

3. Most of the respondents are not in favour of any violent uprising to topple the existing system;

4. They are preoccupied with their daily wages, and have no time to get organized for any violent protest;

5. Sometimes they join protest rallies at the insistence of political parties, but they are mostly ignorant about the issue;

6. Majority of the Indian poor believe in destiny and fate. They think that their ordeal is due to the wish of the Almighty;

7. Most of them want to be rich through hard work, although some want to be rich by any means;

8. Almost ninety per cent of the respondents (89.3%) were unsure about how democracy worked in India, but preferred to vote in all elections;

9. Most of them heard about Priti G, but did not know about her official designation;

10. Most of them heard about Moti Barman, but did not know his designation;

11. They feel proud when they cast their vote in elections;

12. Most of them heard about famous film stars and cricketers, but had seldom seen their films or matches;

13. Most of them are afraid of police and custody, because these may affect their daily wage;

14. Nearly thirty five per cent of the married respondents send their children to school;

15. They want their children to be educated, and become government employees;

16. Majority of them are proud to be Indians, and believe that India is a great country and a big military power;

17. They are not always grumbling with the way they live.

J wrote in the footnote that this were his findings after a survey with a very small group of people, one hundred and ten to be exact, and the findings must not be taken as final and conclusive. His findings might vary with a bigger and comprehensive survey. He also wrote that the poor he surveyed included the illiterates as well. Regarding the poor persons' love for India, J wrote: "This reminds me of my love for my own mother, a lady who could not afford education for her children, a mother who did not care for her daughters, a person who was a refugee, a person bound by many limitations; an inconsistent lady full of flaws. Yet I love her, I love my mother".

The Khalistan leader and his supporters, who took shelter at a holy shrine, were killed in 'Operation Golden Moon', carried out by security forces under orders from the central government. Life in Punjab was affected for a few days, but gradually limped back to normalcy. Life had its own dynamics. The grueling summer was replaced by a comfortable autumn. In this part of the country, Durga Puja came and went and J visited his hometown and came back early to the hostel. J wrote his survey 'findings' during Puja holidays, when the university was closed. Now the classes had started again after long holidays. J's survey was finally over; he could now concentrate on his studies. The survey shattered many myths about the Indian poor: angry, rebellious, cursing nature of the Indian poor. But now, J wanted to forget about his survey. Exams were not far off, and J had to cover many unattended areas of the syllabus. Classes were going on in full swing. Professors were also keen to finish their assignments.

The news reached J's university at around 2.30 pm. Priti Gautam was shot dead in her official residence by two security persons in retaliation to the 'Operation Golden Moon'. The whole nation, including the city, came to a standstill. People were tense; reports of sporadic violence in different parts of the country started to reach this city. Public transports were off the streets. Students and office-goers had to walk long miles to reach home. It was a black Wednesday. Three days later, J and the whole nation watched on television, Priti G's last rites. Her eldest son performed the last rites and took the rounds around the funeral pyre. J visualized himself as Priti G's eldest son performing the last rites. Death, despair and black smoke engulfed him again, several years after a sultry summer in 1969. Communal riots were reported from northern India, mainly from Delhi. Funeral processions started from almost every home and surrounded almost every part of the motherland, J thought as he started preparing (selfishly) for his exam. Unlike earlier times, this examination won't be deferred. There was no war, but this peace-time had produced many more funeral processions, - much longer, silent and unnoticed funeral processions in the motherland. Poor people's beloved motherland, called India.

Schools, colleges and offices reopened after five days. Life became normal. The Bengal government handled the situation efficiently, and controlled well public outbursts of passion and anger. Classes resumed at J's university as well. Girls' Common room became functional with a TT Board; posters of 'victory' of a particular students' organization could be seen everywhere in the university. Life had a unique capacity to survive. J now studied mostly at night, to fill up the earlier lapses. He wanted to do well at the exam. The hostel remained silent, almost dead at night. It was the ideal time for study. Therefore, J loved to study at night. He often fell asleep in his bed while studying, and woke up late next morning, and rushed to the university. He was keen to do well at the ensuing examination.

At one of such dead nights, a tired and exasperated J abandoned his studies and headed for the hostel ground. He took his bed-cover and lay on it in the ground. Stars greeted him there. The sky was unusually clear this night, and all the stars were astonishingly visible in the city-sky this night! Dim moonlight created a mystique, magical atmosphere. It took J back to his childhood days. The small hostel ground suddenly became very big, - like the cricket ground of his home-town. In that huge ground, there was no 'mahalaya' cricket, but a very big piece of cloth that covered the whole ground. J went closer. A gigantic map of India was painted on the cloth. J saw many people around the map of India. They were going around the map in that huge ground. J realized that they all joined funeral processions, thousands of people were walking in several funeral processions, around India. J saw mourners of Tarachand's death in the procession; mourners of Priti G's death; hundreds of Sikh families had joined the procession; Muslims, Christians, Buddhists, Jains had also joined the procession. Many graves had been dug up in different corners of the ground, many pyres prepared. J also joined the procession, and murmured "Balo Hari, Hari Bol... Balo Hari, Hari Bol"... But his voice was silenced by shouts of "Mera Bharat Mahan", "Jai Ho India" and "Bharat Mata ki Jai"; - people in funeral processions were loudly chanting these new 'mantras'. J felt uncomfortable. He had never seen, never heard any loud cheer in funeral processions. Whose India was it? J looked up to the sky in desperation. There he saw, - for the first time in his life, his paralytic father waving from among the stars, with a cryptic smile on his face.

J silently slipped out of the exuberant, excited, cheering crowd. And fell asleep.

*　　*　　*